SATELLITE OF DOOM

Interior illustration by Guido Guidi

This book is a work of fiction. Names, characters, places, and incidents are the product of the authors' imaginations or are used fictitiously. Any resemblance to actual events, locales, or persons, living or dead, is coincidental.

Little, Brown and Company

Hachette Book Group
237 Park Avenue, New York, NY 10017
Visit our website at www.lb-kids.com

Little, Brown and Company is a division of Hachette Book Group, Inc.
The Little, Brown name and logo are trademarks of Hachette Book Group, Inc.

The publisher is not responsible for websites (or their content) that are not owned by the publisher.

First Edition: September 2013

Library of Congress Cataloging-in-Publication Data

Windham, Ryder.
Satellite of doom / by Ryder Windham and Jason Fry. — 1st ed.
p. cm. — Transformers classified ; [3])
ISBN 978-0-316-18869-2
I. Fry, Jason, 1969– II. Title.
PZ7.W72433Sat 2013
[Fic]—dc23 2012049763

10 9 8 7 6 5 4 3 2 1

RRD-C

Printed in the United States of America

SATELLITE OF DOOM

BY RYDER WINDHAM
AND JASON FRY

CONTENTS

Chapter One
BLUE PLANET

It didn't take long for the two wolves to find the body.

Moving deftly through the narrow ravine, the predators kept to the shadows, staying out of the light of the blue sun. They were creatures of darkness; they had wiry coats, spiky tails, and sharp claws, and their wide jaws were stained with dark, oily blood.

The smaller wolf sprang atop a crag and sniffed at the air, its eyes glowing like orange sparks. The larger one flattened its ears and snarled at its companion, who slunk down, waiting to be led through the twists and turns. The two moved around piles of rocks that had fallen and were now carpeted with dull red moss, then took cover behind a cluster of tall, tubular purple growths that were swollen with water.

The larger wolf had one clawed forefoot slightly raised when its whole body froze. Ahead, in the center of the ravine, it saw a lone human, lying motionless. The wolf took several sniffs, analyzing the rich soup of scents, then growled. Both predators were eager to sink their teeth into their helpless prey, to drain its body of nourishment and energy.

They sprang forward, their jaws opening to reveal black, razor-sharp teeth. They were only a few strides away from their meal when it moved, lifting its head as it yelled, "NOW!"

Sergeant Duane Bowman flung himself sideways, ignoring the pain that shot up through his left leg. He held out a knife, ready to fight. But before he could, a wire net sailed out from beyond the surrounding rocks and fell over the wolves. The beasts snarled and struggled as four other U.S. Army soldiers scrambled down the walls of the ravine.

As Duane pushed up from the ground, he kept his eyes on the wolves and a tight grip on his knife. The smaller one had been caught in the center of the trap, but the larger was already working its head and one leg free. It turned its blazing eyes on Duane and snarled.

Duane shouted, "Cobb! Anson!"

Corporal Cobb, a dark-skinned man, seized one edge of the net and dragged it back over the smaller wolf so it couldn't escape. Corporal Anson, a thin man with a rash of freckles across his face, raced over to jab a spear of jagged metal into its tough hide. The creature snarled, its jaws snapping. As Cobb clutched the net and Anson continued his attack, Duane moved toward the other creature and shouted, "Rose! McVey!"

From the other side of the ravine came two more soldiers, their own spears at the ready. Corporal Rose was short and stocky. Corporal McVey was tall with broad, muscular shoulders. They thrust their spears through the net and jabbed the larger wolf. The impact of McVey's spear sent a spray of sparks up toward his head, startling him and causing him to stumble backward.

The smaller wolf screeched. Its companion howled, threw off the net, and sprang at Anson, moving with surprising speed. Duane lunged for its hindquarters, but his leg buckled under him, and he tumbled to his knees. Anson didn't move fast enough to stop the creature's teeth from locking into his arm. He screamed and reached for the wolf's throat as Duane and Cobb grabbed it. Duane drove an elbow into the back of its head, causing its jaws to pop open and release Anson's arm.

Anson used his good arm to drive his spear through the wolf's neck, sending more sparks flying. The creature collapsed, twitched once, and then went still. While the other four soldiers stood nearby, gasping for breath, Duane reached out cautiously to the side of the wolf's body, pushing his fingers past the wire-like hair. He couldn't feel a trace of warmth.

Duane turned to Rose and said, "Keep your eyes peeled for other ones."

"Yes, sir," Rose said.

Duane eyed Anson and saw nasty-looking

punctures in the man's forearm. Duane asked, "Are you okay?"

"It's nothing, Sarge," Anson said, clutching his injury.

Duane noticed Anson looked pale. He nodded at McVey and said, "Patch him up."

"Yes, sir," McVey said as he moved toward Anson.

Cobb knelt beside the larger wolf.

"Sir, look at this," he said.

Duane hobbled over, wincing at the pain in his ankle. A few days earlier, he'd sprained or broken it in a tumble down a slope of loose rock and set it in a makeshift splint. He eased himself down beside Cobb, who had pushed back the wiry fur to expose the hide. The soldiers' spears had pierced the wolf's tough hide in numerous places.

"No blood," Cobb said.

Duane reached into one of the creature's wounds and pulled out a loose bunch of cables and metal conduits. Sparks shot out of its mouth as Duane withdrew his arm. The wolf jerked.

"It's a robot," Cobb said. "And here I was looking forward to meat for dinner!"

Duane threw the mechanical innards aside. "I don't think it's a robot," he said. "At least not an ordinary one, the kind built by people. I'm guessing it's Cybertronian."

"Cybertronian?" Cobb said. "But...these things don't look at all like what we fought back on Earth."

"Remember what I told you?" Duane said. "Cybertronians aren't like ordinary robots. They're living creatures, with mechanical parts instead of flesh and bone, and they can change their shape and appearance. They can look like...well, like just about anything."

Cobb nodded. "You also said there were two kinds of Cybertronians."

"That's right," Duane said. "Autobots and Decepticons." Duane glanced at McVey, who had torn off a length of fabric from his own shirt to make a bandage and was busily wrapping it around Anson's arm. Duane continued, "And according to headquarters, the Autobots are on our side."

Cobb said, "Well, then *these* critters must be Decepticons, because the only side they seemed interested in was our insides!"

"Hey, Sarge," McVey said. "Maybe the robot—I mean, the Decepticon—we fought in Nevada...you think maybe he *sent* us here?"

Duane thought back to his squad's last moments on Earth. They had been in combat with a Decepticon, a massive gleaming biped with burning orange eyes, near Hawthorne

Army Depot in Nevada. He remembered that the Decepticon hadn't fired its missiles or cannons at the squad, but it had flung a strange cylinder, which had landed on the ground right in the middle of Duane's men. A moment later, they felt their bodies being pulled toward the cylinder and were suddenly consumed by darkness. When they awoke, they were on the cold world where the sun bathed everything in its eerie blue light. They called it Blue Planet.

"Maybe," Duane said finally. "Maybe the Decepticon sent us here. Fact is, we just don't know. Maybe that big cylinder he threw at us just opened up a wormhole to another dimension, and we fell into it."

"Wormhole?" Cobb said. "You mean, like those time-warp things in science-fiction movies?"

Duane smiled. "I read a lot of science fiction

when I was a kid. Back then, no one imagined that giant living machines might arrive on Earth and drag us into their war. Now, we're on another world. It's anybody's guess if a wormhole got us here, but I know this much... my parents are dead because of the Cybertronians' war, and we are *not* in a movie."

"I'm sorry, sir," Cobb said. "I didn't know about your parents."

Duane sighed. "They were killed in a battle between the Autobots and Decepticons. At first, I blamed all the Cybertronians. Then I learned the Autobots had been doing their best to prevent the Decepticons from harming people. Still...I wish the Cybertronians had never arrived on Earth." He shook his head. "I can't stop wondering how my little brother got mixed up in the fight. And if he's still alive."

Duane sighed again. When he'd last seen

him, Kevin had tried to explain a series of misadventures that had brought him from Hurley's Crossing all the way to Hawthorne. Kevin had said something about chasing a Decepticon named Reverb to a hidden weapons storehouse. But before Duane could make sense of what his brother was saying, the Decepticon attacked, Kevin took cover, and Duane and his squad were almost instantly transported—with no idea how to get home.

Blue Planet's days and nights were short, a little more than fifteen hours from dawn to dawn. The air smelled rotten. Duane lifted his gaze to the sky. Even though the sun had not yet set, other stars were already visible. On Earth, Duane knew several constellations well enough to identify them, but the stars in this sky didn't resemble any configurations he remembered.

Rose raised one hand, signaling everyone

to hold still. Duane followed Rose's gaze to a distant field of tubular flowers. Duane whispered, "More wolves?"

"Maybe not," Rose said. "I thought I saw something move but...might have just been a breeze."

Duane and his squad had discovered that the tube-flowers, when punctured, released small amounts of liquid. For nearly three weeks, they had survived by drinking the liquid and eating the red moss that grew over just about everything. The moss tasted like dried fish; the liquid was sickeningly sweet and weirdly thick, like congealed cough syrup. The soldiers had no way to know whether their food and "water" were entirely safe. All they knew was that the stuff hadn't killed them yet.

The wolves had been stalking Duane's squad since shortly after their arrival. He and his men had slept in shifts; the lookouts kept watch with their backs to the campfire, listening for approaching footsteps in the darkness. They had seen strange tracks that hadn't been left by wolves, and they could only imagine what other creatures were out there, waiting for a chance to swoop in and devour them.

"If they knew we were out of ammo, they'd get on with it," Duane muttered to himself.

"You say something, Sarge?" McVey said as he looked up from bandaging Anson's arm.

"Talking to myself," Duane said. He shook his head and scanned the ravine. The bottom was still largely in shadow. He wanted to get moving, but he didn't know where.

"Sarge?" Cobb said.

"What is it, Corporal?" Duane replied.

"Well, if these things are robots or

Cybertronians or whatever, that's another sign that there's advanced technology on this world."

Rose said, "The only technology I'm interested in right now is the kind that might get us home."

Duane looked at the four soldiers' faces and saw hope fighting against despair and exhaustion. He wondered if his own face showed a similar mix of emotions.

He considered pointing out that the wolves were the only machines they'd seen that actually worked. He also considered reminding them that the alien structures they'd found had been destroyed, useless except as sources of metal and wire. He suspected that whoever had built the ruins was long gone and wondered whether he should share that theory with his men.

But he didn't want to disappoint them. Cobb, Anson, Rose, and McVey were under his command. He was responsible for them, and he'd promised them that they'd return to Earth somehow.

"Come on," Duane said. "We've got to keep moving. Gather up the net and let's move out."

Cobb said, "Where to, Sarge?"

"Back the way we came," Duane said. "Back to the alien ruins—the fort, or whatever it was—and then our arrival point. Maybe we missed something back there.... Something that will help us find our way home."

The soldiers looked at one another. Duane squared his shoulders and barked, "You got that?"

"Sir! Yes, sir!" yelped the four, rushing to gather up the wire net. Duane nodded and turned to look back along the course of the ravine, trying to retrace their route in his mind. He hoped he could remember the way.

And despite his determination to keep his men believing they would escape from Blue Planet, he felt a nagging fear that he would never see his brother again.

Chapter Two
MYSTERIES OF THE PILLAR

Light-years away from Blue Planet, twelve-year-old Kevin Bowman was standing in the somewhat-crowded science lab at NEST's Rapid Response Base, trying not to look as impatient as he felt.

NEST was the acronym for Non-biological Extraterrestrial Species Treaty, the secret military unit established by an agreement between the Autobots and the U.S. armed forces in opposition to the Decepticons and their leader,

Megatron. NEST had facilities scattered around the world, and the Rapid Response Base happened to be housed in a collection of hangars on the northern edge of Nellis Air Force Range in Nevada.

The Rapid Response Base had been Kevin's temporary home since his older brother disappeared during the fight with Reverb. NEST officials had reluctantly agreed that Kevin could live at the base until Duane's fate became clear. Meanwhile, Kevin was expected to stay out of trouble and do the schoolwork given to him by NEST tutors.

Kevin had to admit he hadn't done a particularly good job at either of those things. Even if the subject was math or science, he was still more interested in trying to find his missing brother than studying. And when he had discovered an opportunity to search for clues to help find his brother, Kevin rushed away from NEST, accompanied by the Autobots Bumblebee and Gears, and Douglas Porter—the son of the president and CEO of military contractor Hyperdynamix Laboratories.

Kevin had followed Duane's trail to a Cybertronian storehouse outside the town of Battle Mountain. There, he and Douglas discovered another large metal cylinder like the one that had transported Duane. The cylinder was intact and seemed to be functional, but just being in possession of it didn't bring Kevin any closer to getting Duane back. For all Kevin knew, his brother might already be dead.

Kevin shook his head. He wouldn't allow himself to think that way. He would find a way to save Duane, and they would return to the little house where they'd grown up, where they'd played endless games of pickle with their father, and where their mother had taught them the names of the constellations overhead. Kevin's parents had died, but he wouldn't let the same thing happen to his brother.

"Kevin Bowman? Are you currently receiving auditory input?" asked a deep, booming voice.

Kevin looked up into the metal face of Gears, who had bent down to peer at him with his glowing blue eyes. Behind the Autobot, Chief Lindsay and his technicians were looking curiously at the boy.

"Sorry, everybody," Kevin said. "I'm listening. I just... have a lot on my mind. What were you saying, Chief Lindsay?"

"I was saying that we've traced the power flows inside the cylinder to points here, here, and here," Lindsay said, letting the dot projected from his laser pointer play over the face of the mysterious cylinder they had recovered from the Battle Mountain storehouse.

The cylinder, with four small rectangles of glass and a switch, sat inside a cube of three-inch-thick glass, festooned with sensors meant to detect its activity. Across the lab sat a similar cube with an apparently identical cylinder—the one Reverb had activated at Hawthorne Army Depot. The only obvious difference between the two cylinders was that the rectangles and switch on the one from Hawthorne had melted into a shapeless mass.

"So," Lindsay continued, "we think we know how the cylinder's activated. You set the coordinates by pressing the rectangles, then use the switch to start a countdown. And now we've learned some things about the internal circuitry, or structure, or whatever it is inside there."

Kevin studied the cylinder. "Well, I guess that's good to know, but...does all that info get us any closer to figuring out where my brother went?"

Chief Lindsay frowned. "Well, I like to think that the more we learn, the closer we'll get."

"I'm sorry, Chief Lindsay," Kevin said. "I know you've been spending all your time on this and you're doing everything you can to help."

Lindsay smiled. "Well, you should know we've learned some other things, too. For example, we've been able to monitor the rate at which certain isotopes in the Hawthorne cylinder are decaying. We compared that data with the video footage Douglas Porter gave us, and we determined, with a reasonable amount of confidence, that Reverb set a very short countdown—probably thirty seconds—before he used the cylinder to make your brother and his squad vanish."

"Which tells us what?" Kevin said impatiently.

Chief Lindsay sighed. "Kevin, everything we learn about the cylinders makes it more likely that we'll eventually figure out how they work. For instance, by mapping the internal circuitry, we may learn if different coordinates require different power levels. If so, we could be able to determine what power levels were experienced by the Hawthorne cylinder and replicate the coordinates entered by Reverb."

Kevin turned to Gears and said, "What do you think?"

"I don't know, Kevin," Gears said in his rumbling mechanical voice. "The pillars are ancient Cybertronian technology, abandoned thousands of years ago. Unfortunately, neither I nor my fellow Autobots know how they worked. However…" Gears took a cautious step closer to the cube, the pistons in his massive legs activating as he bent down to peer through the glass. "Chief Lindsay, how have you mapped the internal circuitry? What is the method of exploration?"

"We send small electric impulses into the cylinder," Chief Lindsay said. "We don't use very much power—not enough to risk activating anything, just enough for our instruments to register where the electricity flows. Think of it like diagnostic impulses running through your sensory conduits, Gears. By monitoring where the impulses travel between, say, your shoulder and your fingertips, we can tell where the conduits in your arm are located and how they're connected. In fact, we're just about set for today's mapping test. Kittridge, are you ready to begin?"

Kittridge, a young scientist with a flattop of red hair, looked up from his computer and nodded.

"Should we wait for Optimus Prime and the others to conduct this test?" Gears asked.

"No need," Lindsay said. "We've conducted more than twenty similar tests so far. And believe me, I keep Optimus and the others well informed of our findings. Besides, Optimus, Ironhide, and Ratchet are all at Hyperdynamix Aerospace with General Marcus for Dr. Porter's rocket launch."

"Let's do it," Kevin said.

Lindsay nodded to Kittridge, who typed commands into his laptop.

"Impulse actuator coming online," the young man reported. "Power levels at thirty percent. Now fifty percent."

Kevin leaned forward until his forehead was almost against the glass cube. He heard a mechanical whine as Gears leaned forward, too. Lindsay glanced at Kevin and Gears and smiled as he said, "If you're expecting to see anything happen to the cylinder, I don't believe you will."

"Sixty-five percent," Kittridge stated.

Gears said politely, "May I remind you, Chief Lindsay, that my vision extends into the ultraviolet and infrared spectrums?"

"That won't matter," Lindsay replied. "We're only sending a small bit of electricity down the circuits. Heating would be minimal, even if—"

Kittridge interrupted, "Topping seventy-five percent."

Kevin gasped. The rectangles on the undamaged cylinder were glowing.

"One hundred percent," Kittridge said.

The cylinder's rectangles glowed brighter

and then began flickering rapidly. Lindsay ordered, "Get me a power reading."

"We didn't do anything different!" Kittridge exclaimed.

Kevin asked, "What's going on?!"

Kittridge said, "Power levels have climbed to six hundred percent!"

One rectangle stopped flickering. It displayed a strange symbol that reminded Kevin of a cluster of sticks. He pointed to the symbol and said, "Gears, do you recognize that?"

"Yes," Gears said. "It is an ancient form of a Cybertronian numeral. In our language, we call it..." Gears emitted an extraordinarily loud chirp.

Kevin, Lindsay, and Kittridge clapped their hands over their ears. Feeling like his skull was going to split open, Kevin gasped, "Did you have to say it so loud?"

"I'm sorry," Gears said. "That's the only way to pronounce it."

"Look!" Lindsay said. The cylinder's second rectangle displayed a different symbol.

Gears pointed to the second symbol and said, "In Cybertronian, we call that—"

"NO!" Kevin and Kittridge yelled at the same time. Kevin added, "Not out loud!"

Gears drew his head back in surprise. "Oh."

Chief Lindsay kept his eyes on the cylinder as he said, "I don't know how or why, but it appears the sequence code has started." He continued, "When the entire code's loaded into the pillar, it will activate."

"And pull us into a wormhole," Kevin said, backing away hastily from the glass and tripping over a thick power cable.

Trying to keep his voice calm, Lindsay said, "We need to get out of here. Now."

The third rectangle displayed a new symbol.

"Move!" Lindsay yelled. "Go!"

Kevin scrambled to his feet and ran. As they all raced to the doors that led out of the lab, Kevin glanced back and saw Gears still staring at the cylinder.

"Gears! Get out of there!"

Kittridge reached the exit first and shoved open the doors, startling the two NEST guards who were stationed outside. The soldiers fumbled for their machine guns as Lindsay screamed at them to run. It was only when the soldiers saw the thirteen-foot-tall Autobot stomping toward them that they turned and raced to catch up.

As Kevin ran through the corridor, he wondered if they would all be able to get far enough away from the cylinder to avoid the pull of the wormhole. He expected to hear a roar of imploding equipment from the lab behind them, then a rush of air into the hole in space-time as the ancient machine's gravity clawed at him and dragged him backward.

He was halfway down the corridor before he realized he hadn't heard anything.

Kevin stopped running. Lindsay plowed into him from behind and knocked him over. Lindsay stopped fast, grabbed Kevin's arm, and yanked him up from the floor. "Keep running!" Lindsay said, gasping for air.

"Wait!" Kevin said. "Chief Lindsay, the cylinder didn't activate!"

Still trying to catch his breath, Lindsay looked back over his shoulder and saw that Kittridge and the two soldiers had come to a halt as well. Gears drew to a stop behind them. Lindsay said, "You're right. That's...strange."

"Sir?" one of the soldiers asked. "What's happening, sir?"

"I have no idea," Chief Lindsay muttered. "Come on, Kittridge."

The soldiers looked at each other and shrugged as the two scientists walked back down the corridor, followed by the boy and the Autobot.

Returning to the lab, they found the cylinder still inside the glass cube. All four rectangles on the cylinder displayed Cybertronian numbers.

Kevin said, "Why didn't it activate?"

"Maybe it malfunctioned," Kittridge said. "The cylinder was lying beneath a mountain for ages. Maybe dust, dirt, and time had a combined bad effect on it."

"Perhaps," Lindsay said. "I wonder if—Kittridge! See if you can get a reading on the levels of isotope decay."

"Yes, sir," Kittridge said, sitting down and tapping at his laptop. After a moment he nodded. "Definite signs of breakdown."

"Get me a decay rate," Lindsay said. "Then compare it to the decay rate from the Hawthorne pillar. And extrapolate the countdown time."

"Calculating now," Kittridge said. "Got it. The Hawthorne video is missing the moment when the Decepticon activated the pillar, so the math won't be exact. But my best estimate would be... four-point-two days."

"Fascinating," Lindsay said.

"What's fascinating?" Kevin said. "Why didn't the cylinder activate?"

Gears cleared his mechanical throat, and then said, "I believe Chief Lindsay is saying it *did* activate, Kevin. Or, more precisely, the countdown to activation has begun.... Only it is a much longer countdown than Reverb used in the confrontation at Hawthorne Army Depot."

"That's correct," Lindsay said. "But why did the new cylinder activate? Maybe our test impulses primed it. In any event, the countdown has begun."

Kevin said, "You mean, in a little over four days, it will create another wormhole?"

"Yes," Lindsay said. "That's precisely what I mean."

Kevin realized his hands were trembling, and he shoved them in his pockets. "But you don't know whether the wormhole will lead us to my brother, do you?"

Lindsay smiled. "Let me and Kittridge get back to work, Kevin, and trust I will do what I can to answer that question before four-point-two days from now."

Kevin glanced at Kittridge and saw fear in the man's eyes. Gears gently patted Kevin's shoulder and said, "Perhaps we should move to a safer location."

"No," Kevin said. "That cylinder may be Duane's only ticket home. I'm not letting it out of my sight!"

Chapter Three

DR. PORTER'S ROCKETS

"Aren't they beautiful?" said Dr. Alexander Porter as he gazed at two tall needle-nosed rockets, each bearing a logo of a large red H on the side. The logo represented Porter's primary company, Hyperdynamix Laboratories.

"Your rockets are impressive displays of technology," Optimus Prime replied politely. Porter had long gray hair and horn-rimmed glasses and was wearing his usual white lab coat. Optimus Prime was the towering, powerful leader of the Autobots and had blue armor decorated with red flames. He was accompanied by his allies Ironhide and Ratchet. Ironhide was the weapons specialist with a black-and-silver chassis pitted with scars from countless battles. Ratchet, the Autobots' medical officer, had a retractable buzz saw contained within his left arm.

Ironhide leaned toward Optimus and muttered, "You think the rockets are impressive? Are you kidding? By Cybertronian standards, those things aren't even kid stuff."

Optimus ignored the comment. The Autobots stood near Dr. Porter and General Marcus, a tanned older man with bright blue eyes. Marcus's aide stood behind him along with six NEST officers. All faced the two rockets. Each rocket sat atop a trio of conical jet nozzles and rested at the center of an immense circular underground launch facility. The complex lay one hundred feet below a fold of the Spring Mountains west of Las Vegas and Mission City and behind rings of electric fences patrolled by both human guards and remote-controlled drones. Directly above the rockets, embedded in the complex's ceiling, was a sealed metal hatch, seventy feet in diameter. Attached to each rocket was a Reusable Launch Vehicle the size of a pickup truck.

Ratchet said, "I kind of like the way the RLVs are attached to the rockets. Reminds me of babies clinging to their mothers."

Optimus only glanced at his allies, but it was enough to encourage Ironhide and Ratchet to keep their remarks to themselves. He turned his attention to the Hyperdynamix Aerospace technicians who rushed about the chamber, talking into their headsets as they typed on tablet computers and inspected the rockets' fuel linkages and the complex's ventilation systems.

Optimus had deactivated his auditory sensors' noise-canceling algorithms a tenth of a second after he'd taken his first step into the launch chamber. He could hear everything, from the tiny sound of valves opening and closing inside the rocket to the worried whisper of a technician who wanted desperately to visit the nearest restroom.

Just then, Douglas Porter entered the launch chamber. The boy's blond hair was perfectly groomed, and he carried a leather briefcase.

Dr. Porter turned to General Marcus and the other NEST officers and said, "We have three RLVs built, with three more in production. RLV-1 is in orbit now, with the Hyperdynamix Orbital Debris Disposal Initiative Station, or HODDIS for short. The RLVs before us are

RLV-2 and RLV-3." Porter pressed a switch on a console that activated a tall retractable blast shield. The shield rumbled out from an enormous slot in one wall and moved between the two rockets. "The blast shield," Porter continued, "protects one RLV from the other during launches, and enables us to launch both RLVs within minutes of each other. The crew cabins in each RLV can accommodate three astronauts for manned missions, but most orbital tasks can be performed by the RLVs' onboard artificial intelligence."

General Marcus frowned. "You're a technological wizard, Doctor. That's obvious. But I have my doubts about your artificial intelligence systems. Robots can do astonishing things, but what do they do when a situation arises that isn't in their programming? Can they improvise?" Remembering the three hulking

Autobots, Marcus turned to them, spread his arms peaceably, and added, "No offense meant, of course."

"No apology is necessary," Ratchet said. "As you know, General, we are not robots, but autonomous organisms."

Douglas Porter cleared his throat. "Father, may I answer the general's question?"

Dr. Porter nodded. "Very well, Douglas."

Douglas smiled and showed off his perfect white teeth. "General, I think you'll agree that when we talk of improvisation, we rarely if ever mean that we're trying something completely unknown, with no idea about the results. More often, we mean that we're switching from a standard method of solving one problem to another, or reclassifying the problem as something else. And artificial intelligences can certainly do that. Each RLV's AI is programmed for more than twenty-seven thousand different situations. So yes, General, the AI *can* improvise."

"That will do, Douglas," Dr. Porter said. "And now, gentlemen, please follow me to the control room. I'm told they're about ready for us aboard the HODDIS. The elevator is this way, and it's big enough to accommodate Autobots."

Ironhide flexed his arms, gears and pistons whirring and rattling as his metal fists recalibrated themselves into deadly cannons. "That's good news about the elevator, Doc," he rumbled. "I'd hate to hafta make some modifications to your place here."

Dr. Porter scowled and shook his head. Optimus Prime turned and gave Ironhide another warning look, but the weapons specialist merely grinned.

Chapter Four

SPACE MISSION

High above Earth, sunlight flashed off the curved solar panels and communications dish on the Hyperdynamix Orbital Debris Disposal Initiative Station. The HODDIS was an assembly of bulky modules that had been bolted together by industrial robots and resembled a cluster of white trailers. A single RLV was attached to the docking port on the side of the station that faced Earth.

The three astronauts aboard the HODDIS shared a space about the size of a school bus. Commander Gent, Pilot Donnelly, and Science Pilot Hayes worked at separate consoles, with straps keeping them in their padded seats. They wore spacesuits but worked without their helmets, which were tethered to the backs of their seats.

"HODDIS," a voice boomed over the station's speakers. "This is Base One. Do you read?"

Recognizing the flight controller's voice, Commander Gent replied into his headset, "Got you loud and clear, Lyons. We're about halfway through today's cleanup effort."

"Copy that, Gent," Lyons responded. "Stand by for Dr. Porter."

"Oh?" Gent said. The three astronauts exchanged surprised looks.

"Greetings, HODDIS," Porter said. "We've got some visitors down here who are curious about what you're doing. Commander Gent, can you tell our guests about your mission?"

"Roger that, Dr. Porter," Gent said. "For decades, Earth's orbit has been filling up with space junk, everything from discarded rocket stages to dead satellites. One might not think it's a problem with so much room up here, but eventually things break down and even crash into one another. And once that happens, you've got lots of bits and pieces spinning around in orbit. A piece of metal or ceramic moving at high speed can punch a hole in a solar panel or even a station like HODDIS. So Hyperdynamix decided to do something about it."

"Indeed I did," Porter said. "So what exactly are the three of you doing up there right now?"

"Well, Doctor," Gent said, "I'm programming RLV-1 to scour an area for fragments of a Chinese satellite that broke up five years ago. The RLV will deploy its magnetic mesh screens to collect the smaller bits of junk for disposal back home. The bigger stuff gets taken care of by Donnelly and Hayes."

"And how do they do that?" Porter asked.

Gent said, "If your visitors look at the feed from our external cameras, you'll see black spheres below us. Those are solar-powered drones that continuously scan the area and report if they spot potential collisions or any debris we miss. Plus we use them to bump debris down into Earth's gravity well, so the debris burns up during reentry to Earth's atmosphere. We're so close that a few bumps typically do the trick. Eventually, we'll have rings of drones around the Earth in various orbital paths, keeping things clean and making sure satellites stay out of one another's way."

"Thank you, Commander," said Porter. "You may continue your work."

On Earth, Dr. Porter handed his headset to the flight controller, and then gestured to the NEST officers and Autobots. "And now, gentlemen," Porter said, "let's adjourn to the conference room. Douglas, wait for us here."

"But Father—" Douglas protested.

"Was some word in my last sentence unclear?" Dr. Porter said, glaring at Douglas. "You will wait here."

Douglas bit his lower lip, and then nodded. "Yes, Father," he said evenly. He sat down at a table in the control room and snapped open his briefcase. "I have homework to do, anyway."

"Then get it done," Porter said. "Now, gentlemen, if you'll follow me..."

Porter led the officers and Autobots out of the control room and down a corridor. The Cybertronians went in single file, ducking their heads to avoid pipes and bundles of cables that hung from the ceiling.

General Marcus said, "Your son is brilliant, Doctor. You must be very proud."

"I suppose he's bright enough," Porter said. "But he's undisciplined, like most young people."

"You call that boy undisciplined?" Marcus said with a chuckle. "Doctor, I've never known any seventeen-year-old who was so smart and focused. Why, when I was his age, I was more interested in getting into trouble than anything else."

Porter responded with a shrug, then came to a stop in front of a tall, thick metal door. "Here we are," he said as he pressed his thumb against a panel beside the door. A light on the panel turned green, and the door slid aside, revealing a windowless room with a large black table. "This is our secure conference room."

Porter led the NEST officers inside. As the Autobots followed, Ironhide grumbled, "They really should've installed taller doorways in this joint."

Porter moved to sit at the head of the table while the others took their seats. The three Autobots squeezed themselves against the wall beside the door. Porter said, "Automated security systems sweep this room for intrusion devices every hour, so trust we can speak freely here. Let's talk about the *real* purpose of the HODDIS project."

"It is not to clean up space debris?" Ratchet

asked. "I find that disappointing. Every responsible civilization we have encountered is scrupulous about cleaning up its trash."

"Oh, Earth orbits are definitely being cleaned up," Porter said. "And I take great pride in that. It will be one of my first gifts to humanity. But the mission has another purpose, one not even our astronauts know about. And that's to create a network of reconnaissance drones that will give us early warning of incoming Cybertronians."

Optimus Prime said, "How do you propose to do that, Dr. Porter?"

"I've developed a database of information about all of our contact with Cybertronians—Autobots and Decepticons alike. Everything from communication protocols to chemical signatures of meteoroids later identified as Cybertronians in transitional form. Our drones are programmed with this information and sophisticated pattern-matching algorithms. Once the network is complete, they'll be able to scan an ever-increasing volume of space for intrusions, transmissions, and other activity. We'll be able to intercept Decepticons within minutes of their arrival on Earth, if not before."

The NEST officers exchanged surprised glances. General Marcus kept his eyes on Porter and said, "How soon could your network be ready?"

"Within a couple weeks," Porter said. "But we're already receiving terabytes of data from our drones in orbit. That data is transmitted directly to Hyperdynamix Aerospace. And, if you like, the data can be sent to NEST headquarters as well."

The NEST officers began talking to one another urgently in low voices. Ironhide stepped away from the wall, looked down at Dr. Porter, and said, "Why keep your plan with the drones a secret from the astronauts?"

"For security," Porter said. "Since they don't know the drones are collecting and transmitting data about Cybertronians, there's no chance any of the astronauts will make a transmission that might attract attention from the Decepticons. The longer they're unaware of our operation, the bigger the advantage we have in the war."

Ironhide made a grinding noise as he shook his metal head. "I don't like keepin' soldiers in the dark about maneuvers."

"Then we must agree to disagree," Porter said, and then he smiled.

Ironhide emitted a noise that, to human ears, sounded like a low squawk. But the other Autobots heard Ironhide say, *"I don't like Porter's smile one bit. It reminds me of Molryus Minor's carnivorous isopods. I fell into a nest of them once."*

Ironhide glanced at Optimus Prime. The Autobot leader's expression remained impassive as he gazed at Porter. Optimus then looked at General Marcus, who kept his own eyes fixed on Porter. Marcus said, "Why do I get the feeling you have something else to tell us, Doctor?"

"Because I do," Porter said. "The work we did compiling our database revealed patterns about Cybertronian transmission frequencies... frequencies used only by Decepticons. The two RLVs you saw on the launch pad? One is carrying a satellite designed to broadcast on those frequencies, and to direct the drones to rebroadcast the signal. The satellite will turn the HODDIS and our drone network into an incredibly powerful transmitter, one that can fry the circuits of every Decepticon on Earth. The second RLV will deploy orbital weapons to defend the satellite."

Optimus Prime said, "Dr. Porter, are you saying...the satellite will shut down *all* the Decepticons in this planetary system?"

Porter smiled. "Yes."

"An' what about the Autobots?" Ironhide boomed, leaning his big, scarred head over the table to stare at Porter. "What about us?"

"You will be unharmed," Porter said, not budging an inch. "Decepticons will be affected. Only Decepticons."

Optimus Prime said, "How do you know that, Doctor? If such a deadly frequency could be transmitted, surely Cybertronians would have discovered it some time ago."

Porter sighed. "Sometimes, Optimus, the

beings we are least able to understand are ourselves."

Ratchet said, "Standard protocol would be to test your technological weapon first. What are your plans for such tests?"

"Such a test isn't possible," Porter said. "The signal will be instantly detectable to any Decepticon. We will get only one shot at ending their tyranny. I intend to make it count."

"That's a huge risk," Marcus said.

"It isn't a risk at all," Porter said. "It's an opportunity. A huge one."

The NEST officers began muttering to one another. Ratchet and Ironhide exchanged concerned squawks.

Optimus Prime's deep, resonant voice cut through the tumult. "Not every Decepticon is evil," he said. "Some are merely misguided, led astray by Megatron's lies. A universal death sentence is wrong."

Porter said, "You wouldn't accept the death of a few misguided Decepticons to kill hundreds who clearly deserve it?"

Marcus's aide said, "*I'd* accept that."

"I would not," Optimus said. "Dr. Porter, over our long journey to Earth we reviewed millions of broadcasts your planet has pumped out into space over the last few decades. Those broadcasts taught us your belief systems as well as your languages. You are familiar, no doubt, with the Judeo-Christian scriptures, the story of Abraham negotiating with God over the fate of the city of Sodom?"

Porter gave no reply, but a slight grimace suggested he was annoyed by the question.

"I'm familiar with the story," General

Marcus said. "God agreed to spare the city if Abraham could find fifty righteous men among the wicked. Abraham bargained with God, until eventually God agreed to spare the city if Abraham could find ten righteous men."

"Yes," Optimus said, "that is my understanding of the story."

Marcus smiled pleasantly. "Can't say I ever imagined I'd be talking scripture with a giant robot."

"The universe can be a surprising place," Optimus said.

"I know my scripture, too," Porter snapped. "Let me remind you how the story ends. Abraham couldn't find ten righteous men, and so the city was destroyed. This isn't Sunday school, gentlemen. Persuasion and preaching won't save us. My satellite, however—"

Chirp-chirp-chirp, went something in the

pocket of Porter's lab coat. Porter reached into the pocket, pulled out a silver cell phone, held it up to his ear, and said, "This better be important."

One of General Marcus's aides reached for his own phone. The aide listened to his phone, brow furrowing.

"What's going on?" Ratchet asked Optimus Prime.

The Autobot leader was constantly scanning communications from all around the world, including messages sent across NEST's networks. After listening for a moment, he replied, "The humans have detected four meteors. All four are on a direct approach to Earth."

Pistons whirred in Ironhide's arms as he thought of fighting another wave of Decepticon invaders. He said, "Are the incoming objects Cybertronian?"

"Unknown," Optimus said.

Porter put down his phone. So did Marcus's aide, who said, "General, we have a report—"

"Four large meteors," Porter interrupted as he moved to a keyboard at a control station in the center of the conference room. "I'll put them on-screen."

Porter was still tapping at the keyboard as Optimus rumbled, "Heading 859.25, angle 38 degrees below ecliptic. They have just passed the orbit of the Moon."

"That's impossible," Marcus said. "Our long-range satellites would have seen them before they cleared Jupiter. Four large meteors can't have come out of nowhere!"

Porter stopped typing, and a massive screen on the far wall came to life. Earth appeared as a bright blue circle in the center of the screen, and four red arrows became visible, each heading toward Earth. Porter frowned and tapped at his keyboard again. Half the screen went blank before it flickered back on with a view from the HODDIS.

Porter barked, "Commander Gent, this is Base One. Come in, Gent."

"Roger, Base One," Gent replied, his voice piped into the conference room's speakers.

Porter said, "We have four meteors inbound, close to your position. I'm sending you the tracking data now."

A moment later, Gent said, "We've got the data, Doctor. One of your meteors is coming right at us... gonna be close. Too close! Donnelly! Hayes! Stand by the thruster controls. Donnelly, give me a three-second burn."

The meeting room's speakers seemed to

tremble as the astronaut named Donnelly activated the station's engines to lift the HODDIS into a higher orbit.

Gent yelled, "Whoa!"

General Marcus pointed to the side of the screen that displayed the view from the station. A ball of fire shot past the camera, striking one of the drones, which tumbled toward Earth. Bits of metal trailed behind the shattered drone. The ball of flame vanished against the blue bulk of the planet below.

Gent said, "We're fine, Base One," and then he whistled. "Missed us by maybe ten meters."

"Roger that," Porter said. "Base One out."

"Do you think the station was targeted?" Marcus asked.

"I don't know," Porter said. "But the drones' instruments recorded the chemical signature of the four meteors as they passed by. Data is coming up now." He examined a readout. "Hmm. Strange."

"What is it, Doctor?" asked Optimus Prime. "Is it Cybertronian?"

"Yes...and no," Porter said with a frown.

Ironhide said, "Ain't got time for riddles, Doc. Which is it?"

"It has certain characteristics in common with Cybertronian meteoroids," Porter said. "But only certain characteristics. It's unlike any chemical signature I've seen."

General Marcus's aide was on his phone again. He said, "Keep us posted," then pocketed the device. Facing Marcus, he continued, "NEST estimates touchdown will be in northern Idaho. All four meteoroids will land within a three-mile area."

"Alert the proper authorities," Marcus said. "And scramble a commando team."

Optimus said, "We will rendezvous with the commandos." Turning for the doorway, he said, "Autobots, roll out!"

Chapter Five

NIGHT FLIGHT

Douglas Porter stopped pretending to do his homework when his father reentered the control room.

Douglas asked, "Everything go okay with your meeting, Father?"

"Well enough," Porter grumbled.

"What happened—" Douglas began, but his father waved for him to be silent.

Porter spent the next several minutes giving

orders for the technicians to relay to the HODDIS. When he was finished, he glanced at Douglas and said, "What were you pestering me about?"

"Nothing, Father," Douglas said.

Porter glanced at one of the books that rested on the table in front of Douglas. "Aren't you done with that homework yet?"

"It's calculus," Douglas said. "I like it, but it's my hardest subject."

"I loved calculus," Porter said distractedly as he stared over the mission controller's shoulder at a monitor. "Always found it easy."

"Maybe," Douglas said hesitantly, "you could help me with it for a minute?"

Porter glared at his son. "Help you?" His face went red with restrained anger. "You know I don't have time for that. Why do you think I'm paying the best tutors in Nevada? Ask them!"

Douglas lowered his gaze to the cover of his calculus book. "Yes, sir," he said quietly. "Unless you need the helicopter, may I take it back to the house?"

"That's what it's for," Porter said as he turned and walked away.

Twenty minutes later, the teenager was sitting alone in the enclosed cabin of a Hyperdynamix helicopter, high over the mountains of Nevada. He turned on his sleek silver notebook computer and pulled up a video. It showed his father, the NEST officials, and the Autobots in the conference room at Hyperdynamix Aerospace. Douglas laughed as his father boasted about the room's automatic security systems. Douglas had helped create the security systems, and he could bypass them whenever he liked.

Douglas listened to the meeting, waiting to hear if anyone would say anything surprising. No one did. He had known all about the dual purpose of the satellite network from the beginning, just as he'd known about his father's determination to destroy every Decepticon on Earth.

He rewound the video and listened to his father's brag about the first of his gifts to humanity. Douglas snickered and shook his head. Yes, Alexander Porter wanted to win the war against the Decepticons. But it wasn't out of any sense of patriotism or humanity.

Douglas thought, *My father wouldn't care if half the world burned.*

He knew what his father really wanted was to win the war so that Hyperdynamix could gain a monopoly on the production of military and industrial robots, robots he would secretly outfit with spy gear, which would give him access to invaluable data from numerous government agencies.

He wants to rule the world, Douglas thought. *But I won't let him.*

His father had never thanked him for anything. Never complimented him and never treated him as anything more than an inconvenience. Douglas was determined to stop his father, not by tattling on him to NEST or some other ineffectual group, but by ruining his schemes. He wondered what his father's face would look like when he realized all his plans had been ruined. Douglas considered whether he would ever reveal the truth, and let the great Dr. Porter know his own son had outsmarted him. He thought he might get more satisfaction by letting his father spend the rest of his life wondering how everything had gone so wrong.

Douglas smiled. All his plans were coming together. He had his own Decepticon followers, led by the ruthless Reverb, and he had twelve autonomous tanks from Hyperdynamix headquarters near Mission City. The tanks served as his robotic eyes and ears, gathering data on almost everything at Hyperdynamix, and in parts of NEST's bases, too.

And then there was Project Nightbridge.

Douglas tapped at his keypad, entering the password that gave him access to the folder where he kept his most secret files. He played another video, an older one. It showed the fight between Reverb and U.S. Army units at Hawthorne Army Depot, the fight in which Reverb had activated a mysterious ancient cylinder and triggered a wormhole that captured several soldiers, including Kevin Bowman's brother. Douglas froze the video and looked at the Cybertronian numbers visible on the cylinder's readout. He believed the cylinder was a teleportation device, and that the readout indicated where the device had sent the luckless soldiers.

Douglas knew how badly Kevin would want to see this, but he wasn't ready to share the data. He wanted to know the secrets of that ancient Cybertronian technology first.

Douglas glanced at the time and estimated that he'd be in the air for another half hour or so, long enough for him to check on Kevin and what was happening at NEST's Rapid Response Base. When he had last seen Kevin in Mission City, Douglas had brushed up against him and slipped a tiny surveillance robot onto his sleeve. The robot had hidden itself on Kevin's clothes and waited until its built-in geolocator indicated it was within the NEST base. Then the tiny robot had skittered free, making its way to the base's science lab, where NEST kept the cylinder they'd found at Battle Mountain. The robot hiding in the lab had been Douglas's favorite spy ever since.

Douglas activated the video feed from his spybot, fast-forwarding through several boring hours of scientists sitting before their monitors until he saw Kevin walk in, along with the Autobot Gears.

A moment later, Douglas froze the playback, reversed it, and watched in fascination.

"Well, well, well," he murmured to himself. "Very interesting."

Chapter Six
TEETH IN THE NIGHT

The soldiers made their way across the badlands in the dimming light. Duane squinted at the sky. The temperature was dropping rapidly on Blue Planet, but he was still sweating, trying to ignore the pain in his leg.

"Maybe we ought to stop and rest a minute, Sarge," Cobb suggested.

"That's a negative," Duane said, ignoring Cobb's concerned look. He knew Cobb was worried about him and afraid he was pushing himself too hard. But they all had bigger problems, such as the setting sun.

Duane gasped, "Have to find a defensible place... to camp." He pointed ahead.

Cobb, Anson, McVey, and Rose looked to see a bare outcropping that rose above the broken plains. Duane said, "If we can reach those rocks before nightfall, we'll have..." He took a deep breath. "We'll have an elevated position... be able to see any predators coming and... keep them at bay."

Rose said, "That's not where we camped before."

"I know," Duane said. "But it'll do. We just have to get there... before dark. Before those wolves get up their courage and move in."

Duane began shuffling toward the outcropping. The others followed. The thought of more wolves made all the soldiers move faster. Anson stumbled in the gloom and cried out as he hit his wounded arm on the thick dried stalk of a tube-flower.

McVey helped Anson up and said, "You all right?"

"Yeah," Anson said, "but... I thought I saw two flashes of light beyond those rocks. Maybe they were a wolf's eyes."

Cobb looked anxiously from the outcropping ahead to the rapidly diminishing arc of blue light at the horizon. He then looked nervously at McVey. McVey said, "Are we gonna make it?"

"Of course we are," Cobb said without conviction.

"Tear off some moss as you go," Duane gasped. "Eat while you walk. And refill your canteens. We don't want to have to do it later."

"You just keep moving, Sarge," Cobb said.

Duane looked at the sky again. It was awash in violet and green, and the sun was now just a sliver of blue. Feeling exhausted, Duane had to fight the temptation to stop and take in the sunset's alien beauty. He couldn't allow himself to give up. He knew that being caught in the open after dark would be a death sentence for him and every one of his men.

They were within a hundred yards of the outcropping when two wolves hurtled out of the gloom. The creatures snarled as they launched themselves at Anson and McVey. Anson grunted as he drove his knife into one of the beasts' rib cage, causing it to make a hideous yipping noise. McVey caught the other in the belly with his spear. Sparks flew out of its wounded underside. The wolves rolled across the ground before they scrambled up and fled into the darkness, howling.

"Come on!" McVey screamed defiantly as he ran for the outcropping. The others followed.

As they neared the rocks, Duane yelled, "Cobb! Rose! Watch your flank!"

Three more wolves sprang out from Duane's left, their eyes blazing like embers. Cobb caught one across the snout with his knife, but the second wolf knocked him down and lunged for his throat. Duane kicked the beast in the ribs, causing a bolt of pain to travel through his own leg, as Rose thrust his spear into the third wolf's chest, sending its clawed feet windmilling frantically.

Duane pulled Cobb up from the ground, pointed to the rocks, and yelled, "Cobb, stay with me! The rest of you, climb!"

"Go on, Sarge!" Cobb yelled. "I'll cover you!"

"If I can't climb," Duane said, "go on without me. Nobody is dying while trying to push me up there."

McVey and Rose helped Anson scramble up the outcropping. Cobb and Duane saw more glowing eyes in the darkness and swept their spears back and forth, trying to keep the wolves at bay.

"On three," Duane said. "One...two... THREE!"

Duane and Cobb tossed their spears up to a rocky ledge and then began climbing after their weapons. Cobb moved quickly, but Duane's wounded leg was like a dead weight. Dripping sweat, Duane tried to will his arms to work harder and find the strength to pull himself up out of danger.

"Come on, Sarge!" Cobb urged, reaching for his hand.

Duane grabbed Cobb's hand. Cobb braced himself against a rock, grunting with the effort of dragging Duane up the steep, rocky slope. Loose rock tumbled as Duane tried to find a secure place to plant his foot.

A wolf leaped up from below, teeth bared. Duane felt its teeth clamp shut on his uniform, just above the knee. The beast's claws scrabbled on the rock on either side of Duane's legs. Duane could feel the mechanical carnivore's weight threatening to drag him back down into the darkness, and he knew that if he fell he would die.

The other soldiers were yelling, reaching out, and trying to get a grip on Duane's arms and jacket. They pulled him up, and Duane flopped onto his back on the rocky slope. The wolf was still clinging to his wounded leg, trying to pull him down. Duane's comrades held tight and kept him from falling.

Duane kicked desperately at the wolf with his good leg. He drew back his knee for another kick. The creature dodged the blow, and its chest landed on Duane's foot, the sole of his boot planted against its midsection.

Duane shoved his good leg out as hard as he could. He heard the heavy cloth of his trousers rip, and a moment later the wolf was sailing down from the ledge. The other soldiers pulled Duane the rest of the way up the outcropping, bringing him to a higher ledge. Duane lay back against the ledge and gasped.

Rose grinned and said, "You should know better than to play with the strange doggies, Sarge."

Duane lifted his head and smiled despite

the pain. "It's not my fault no one ever taught them how to play fetch." He sat up carefully. "Anson, help me gather moss. The rest of you keep watch."

While Rose, McVey, and Cobb stood guard with their spears, Duane and Anson pulled moss from the surrounding rocks, made a pile, and lit it with their waterproof matches. The moss burned a dull red light, giving off a musky smell.

"Sarge," McVey said. "You...you wanna look at this."

Duane heard the fear in the corporal's voice. He followed McVey's gaze down into the gloom and felt his heart sink. Wolves were massed below them, a seemingly solid carpet of teeth and wiry hair. As Duane watched in horror, three leaped onto the backs of their pack mates. The wolves on the bottom snapped and snarled at the newcomers, but remained in place while the beasts on their backs looked up. The entire pack began snarling and howling. To Duane's ears, they sounded eager to conclude their hunt.

Anson said, "What are those animals doing? Why are they standing on one another?"

"They're not animals," Duane said. "Those things are more intelligent. Look at them. They're working together, figuring out how to close the distance between them and us."

"We've got to hold this position," Cobb said grimly.

Duane continued watching the pack below. He knew that the best chance of survival for him and his men was to arrange themselves side by side, like a phalanx. But even if they took out ten or twenty of the wolves, eventually exhaustion would get the better of them. He was certain they were doomed, that he'd never see his brother again, and that he would be the first man to die on this miserable planet.

A loud shriek shattered the darkness.

The orange eyes below the soldiers shifted to their right. Duane looked in the same direction and saw dozens of long, weirdly jointed legs illuminated by the red light of the fire.

The wolves began screaming.

"What is it?" Rose yelped. "What is it?!"

Twice the size of a man, the centipede had gleaming silver jaws and segmented legs that ended in knife-like claws. The monster's head, riddled with red pits, looked blank and unfinished. If it had any eyes, Duane could not see them. It made a creaking noise as it moved forward.

Metal, Duane thought. *It's mechanical, too.*

The centipede's head swiveled to face the soldiers. Its jaws clacked. The soldiers stared at it in silent horror. Then a wolf snarled below, and the monster swung its head down, striking the beast with terrifying speed.

Eyes glued to the centipede, Duane said in a low voice, "Quiet. I think it's blind."

The soldiers watched the monster use its head and clawed legs to rip through the wolves below. The creatures fought briefly, then howled and scattered in all directions, yipping in terror as they fled. The centipede began feeding on the dead or near dead.

Duane and the soldiers stood silent and still, barely daring to breathe. They watched the monster for several minutes. It paused a few times to lift its eyeless head and tilt it back and forth, but appeared otherwise focused on devouring its prey.

And then, just as quickly as the centipede had emerged from the darkness, it made a clattering noise as its many legs shifted. Then it was gone. Almost a full minute passed before any of the soldiers dared to speak.

McVey whispered, "What in the name of all that's holy was *that*?"

Chapter Seven

TERROR IN THE TREES

The jet-black NEST copter darted over eastern Washington, following the curves of the Priest River. NEST commandos crouched in the cargo hold, safety lines engaged as they stared down at the forest below. In the center of the copter's high-ceilinged cargo hold stood Optimus Prime, Ironhide, and Ratchet, their metal feet magnetized to the deck.

From a loudspeaker, the pilot's voice

announced, "Estimated time of arrival: six minutes."

"Look sharp, people!" yelled the NEST commander.

Ironhide cycled through his weapons, his forearms changing from cannons to missile launchers to a pair of razor-edged ax heads. Holding up the ax heads for Ratchet to see, Ironhide grinned and said, "That look sharp enough?"

"Calm yourself, Ironhide," Ratchet said. "We don't know what awaits us down there. If the meteoroids delivered Autobots instead of Decepticons, you may not get to sate your regrettably unquenchable thirst for violence."

"Ouch," Ironhide said. "Way to bring a guy down, Sawbones."

Optimus Prime looked to his allies and said,

"I am troubled. Why were the meteoroids not detected until their journey to Earth was all but complete?"

"Perhaps," Ratchet said, "Megatron has discovered some kind of camouflage for meteoroids."

Ironhide looked up from checking the power levels on his pulse cannons and glared at Ratchet with mild annoyance. "One minute you're talkin' like there ain't Decepticons down there, next minute you're sayin' they're some superduper stealth version. You wanna make up yer mind?"

Ratchet sighed. "My purpose is healing injuries, not causing them. Knitting severed conduits together and straightening twisted parts. One day, the long conflict with the Decepticons will be over, and I will be able to leave war aside forever."

Ironhide snorted. "Well, I got a feeling that one day isn't gonna be today, so you'd better—"

"This is not the time for quarrels," Optimus Prime interrupted.

The pilot announced, "Approaching target area. I see a clearing ahead. The impact craters are downslope, perhaps a quarter mile through the trees. Stand by."

"Prepare to disembark," Optimus Prime said. He leaned out through the cargo hold's open hatch. When the NEST copter was about twenty feet off the ground, he sprang from the hatch, quickly followed by Ironhide and Ratchet. The jolt of their landing left Ratchet glad for his knee joints' built-in shock absorbers.

"Lock and load!" Ironhide crowed.

"Must you always be so eager to fight?" Ratchet muttered as his sensors scanned the thick trees that pressed in on all sides of the clearing. Behind the Autobots, a team of NEST commandos descended on cables from the copter. When the commandos were on the ground, the copter rose away and rapidly dwindled into a small dot in the eastern sky. The commandos moved forward in pairs, weapons ready as they took their positions around the Autobots.

"The impact site is directly ahead," Optimus said. "I have mapped it and will take point."

Ironhide looked at Optimus as if he was about to protest the order, but then he moved to the right of the Autobot leader while Ratchet moved to the left. They stomped as quietly as possible down a hillside dense with trees, their pulse cannons ready. Ratchet scanned the surrounding forest, his visual sensors registering dozens of small heat signatures, most of which were moving. He quickly magnified the first ten targets and identified them as birds and other forest animals, racing away from the mechanical intruders as quickly as wings and legs could carry them.

Ratchet was suddenly surprised as his olfactory sensors registered substantial levels of a mix of chemicals, which he found unusual but not unpleasant. He said, "What is that smell?"

"The trees," Optimus Prime said. "They are pines. Their adult leaves are called needles."

Ratchet inhaled deeply. "Sometimes I fail to register what a beautiful world this is."

Ironhide said, "Hey, this isn't a sightseeing expedition!"

"Quiet," Optimus Prime said. "We have an estimated thirty seconds to contact."

The Autobots stepped over a tangle of broken, splintered trees. Beyond the lumber, and for hundreds of yards ahead, the forest looked crushed and chewed. Smoke rose from the far side of the ruined area, but Ratchet's sensors detected no threats.

With the commandos following close behind, the Autobots crossed the impact site rapidly, the fallen trees snapping under their metal feet. They reached an area where the ground was churned up and the dirt had turned to steaming mud. Two depressions lay directly ahead.

"Impact craters," Ratchet said.

In the nearest crater lay two halves of a black metal sphere about ten feet across. The surface of the broken sphere was covered with knobs and bumps.

Ironhide said, "What in the name of the Fifth Baron-Warlord of Polyhex is that?"

"I've never seen anything like it," Ratchet said.

"Neither have I," said Optimus Prime as he

took a step forward, his barrage cannons held in front of him. Ratchet and Ironhide followed. Arriving beside the opened sphere, they found it was full of bright green fibers, some of which had spilled out into the crater.

Ratchet said, "Crash webbing?"

"I do not know," Optimus Prime said.

They proceeded to the second sphere, which they found cracked in half as well. Optimus lifted his gaze and scanned the area. "Two hundred yards to the north, I see two more crashed spheres. Both are also empty."

"Infrared scanners detect no heat trail," Ratchet said. "If these spheres carried passengers, I can't tell which way they went."

A grove of pine trees trembled, and then the Autobots heard a low rumble. Before they could determine the source of the rumbling, the ground erupted around them.

The creatures that exploded up from the ground looked like giant robotic centipedes, with a multitude of whirring clawed legs. One clamped its powerful jaws on Optimus's leg. His piston's sensors, an electronic equivalent of nerves that register pain, fired, alerting Optimus that his metal was being crushed. As Optimus shut off the alerts to avoid being distracted, the centipede whipped its spiked tail around, cracking him in the side of the head and knocking him to the ground. Claws ripped at his chest armor, raising curls of blue paint, and he heard a screech of metal on metal.

As Optimus tried to get to his feet, Ironhide's forearm cannons crackled with fire and Ratchet's buzz saw screamed as it tore into the monster.

Optimus drew back one massive fist and

punched the enemy in the head. It let out an electronic screech so violent it made the NEST commandos collapse and writhe in agony. Optimus flung the robot away, sending it smashing into a shattered tree. The mighty Autobot leaped to his feet and noted that the piston in his lower leg was no longer fully functional.

Exhaust fumes were curling out of Ironhide's cannons, and several large, broken legs from his robot opponent lay on the ground in front of him. Some legs were still twitching. Ratchet grabbed another centipede by the tail and plunged his buzz saw into the metal backbone.

Ironhide saw that Optimus Prime was about to be attacked from behind and shouted, "Boss!"

Optimus turned to see the centipede that

was coiled to strike, its metal head tilted in his direction. He was still raising his arms to defend himself when another centipede crashed against his unprotected back.

"Behind you!" Ironhide added too late, and sent a blast of plasma into the ground, just missing the one Optimus was battling.

Optimus reached around and grabbed the centipede. Its jaws locked down on his wrist, severing some data linkages and cracking a coolant reservoir. He tried to hurl his attacker away, but it remained clamped to his wrist. A loud shock traveled through Optimus's systems, and his limbs seized up. He fell to the ground, his face in the dirt, his arms and legs hammering the earth.

Claws tore at Optimus's back armor, gouging deep furrows into his torso. And then his body went still and his vision went dark.

"What happened?" Optimus Prime said. Turning his head slightly, he saw Ironhide looming over him. Behind his head, he saw the deep blue sky of late afternoon.

Before Ironhide could answer, Optimus rolled up fast on his feet, then saw Ratchet standing nearby, too. Ratchet looked concerned, and one of his arms hung limply against his side.

"The creatures," Optimus Prime said. "What—where did they go?"

"Split up, boss," Ironhide said. "Two went north, two east. One that's heading north is damaged. So's Ratchet. And so are you."

"I am fully operational," Optimus said. Ironhide gave him a skeptical look. Optimus ignored it. He looked to the north and to the east, accessed a map of the region from his memory banks, and began calculating and plotting possible courses for the fleeing centipedes. "The two headed east will cross the river and reach the town of Sagle within twenty minutes," he said. "We cannot allow that to happen. You two head east. Deploy the commandos to protect the town if the creatures get past you."

Optimus turned. Stray pulses of electricity danced along his limbs as he started to walk away, heading north.

"Stop!" Ratchet said. "You have suffered damage, Optimus. Going up against two of those creatures alone is...inadvisable."

"They surprised me," Optimus Prime said without breaking his stride. "I won't let that happen again."

Chapter Eight
NEW ORDERS

It took several hours for Kevin to accept that Chief Lindsay was right, that the Cybertronian cylinder wasn't about to yank them into a vortex and spit them out halfway across the galaxy. The cylinder was still sitting in its glass tomb waiting for the conclusion of its four-day countdown. Lindsay had left the room, but Gears and Kittridge had remained.

Kevin stared at the readout, wondering if the

coordinates were the same as the ones on the cylinder that had dragged his brother and his squad away from Earth. For a moment, he felt some hope. *Maybe all the Cybertronian cylinders are programmed with the same coordinates*, he thought. *Maybe Reverb has never changed them. Perhaps Duane was sent to some Cybertronian prison or a waiting area... like a rest stop in an interstellar highway system. Maybe he and the other soldiers are fine—just waiting for someone to pick them up. Maybe...*

But then Kevin began thinking about Cybertronian mathematics. From what he'd learned, Cybertronians used base-10 numbers, which meant there were ten thousand possible combinations of numbers, and ten thousand different places Duane could have ended up. However, he also knew Cybertronians could survive much harsher conditions than humans could.

Even if Duane did get transported to some kind of galactic rest area, what if it's in the middle of deep space, with no air to breathe? Or...maybe Duane never survived the wormhole. Maybe he never even glimpsed his destination.

Kevin felt his hopes begin to fade away.

Gears, apparently sensing his friend's thoughts, walked over to stand beside him. "Do not worry," Gears said. "We will find your brother."

"I hope so, Gears," Kevin said. "I really do hope so." He looked at Kittridge, who was hunkered over his notebook computer. Kittridge looked up from the screen and gave Kevin a thumbs-up. Kevin nodded gratefully.

The doors to the lab opened and Chief Lindsay entered. His expression was grim.

"What is it?" Kevin asked as the doors closed behind Lindsay. "Something's happened, hasn't it?"

"Yes, it has," Lindsay said. "Now, it's nothing bad, but... well—"

"Just tell us!" Kevin snapped.

Facing Kevin, Chief Lindsay said, "I told General Marcus what happened. He says it's unsafe to keep the cylinder here."

"Why?" Kevin asked. "The cylinder hasn't done anything. I mean... it *won't* do anything for four days. At least, that's what you said, right?"

"Yes, that's what I said," Lindsay said. "And I'm pretty sure I'm correct. But I can't say for certain, and... and that's dangerous, Kevin. There's still so much we don't know."

"Such as?"

"Such as whether both cylinders work in the same way." Lindsay gestured to the cylinder they'd recovered from Battle Mountain. "What if this cylinder transports matter here instead of sending it away? It could serve as a portal for a Decepticon invasion."

Kevin gasped. "You don't really believe that, do you?"

"I don't think it's very likely," Lindsay said. "But General Marcus and his advisors think it's a possibility, and because of that—"

Chief Lindsay was interrupted by a team of NEST workers entering, towing a large metal cart behind them.

"Because of that possibility," Lindsay continued, "General Marcus says the pillar can't stay here. It'll be trucked to a more secure location, a NEST vault near Yucca Mountain. It'll be moved there tonight, under heavy guard. Bumblebee and I will go with it. At Yucca, we'll continue to study the cylinder, and if it activates, it will do so in an empty cavern."

Kevin looked at the workers who were readying the cart for the cylinder. He said, "But don't you think the cylinder should stay here? That moving it is a bad idea? What if moving it speeds up the countdown?"

"Kevin, you're speculating without facts. There's no reason to—"

"Chief Lindsay, please listen," Kevin said. "You said yourself there's a lot we don't know. Until we know whether moving the cylinder might risk any chance of getting my brother home—"

"I'm sorry, Kevin," Lindsay said. "My hands are tied."

Gears looked at Lindsay, then bent down to inspect the scientist's wrists. Turning to Kevin, Gears said, "Chief Lindsay's hands are not bound in any way."

Lindsay smiled sadly. "It's just an expression, Gears," he said. "It means I have my orders." Shifting his gaze to Kevin, he added, "It means *we* have our orders."

Douglas leaned close to his notebook. Thanks to his spybot, he had been able to watch and listen to Kevin's conversation with Chief Lindsay in real time. He switched off the video and audio feeds, then reached to a pocket and extracted a glossy black cell phone. He activated a software program that would change his voice into an electronic drone that couldn't be identified as male or female, young or old, or even human. He then tapped out a phone number he knew by heart. The call was answered on the first ring.

"This is Stealth One," said Simon Clay. "Go ahead, Stealth Leader."

Douglas said, "Are Reverb and the tanks ready?"

"They're ready, Stealth Leader," Clay replied. "We just finished a final test of the command-and-control algorithms. The tanks respond to Reverb's thoughts, his mental commands.... Although I'm not sure it would be accurate to call whatever it is inside his head a brain."

"He does indeed have a brain," Douglas said. "And it's filled with mostly violent thoughts. You'd best not forget that."

"Yes, sir," Clay said sheepishly.

"Prepare the tanks," Douglas said. "We have an intercept mission. Tonight."

"Yes, Stealth Leader," Clay said. "What's the target?"

"A truck convoy," Douglas said as he used his free hand to tap at his computer and upload a map of the area around NEST headquarters. "The trucks will be traveling from the northern edge of Nellis Air Force Range down Highway Ninety-Nine to Yucca Mountain. We'll intercept it north of Beatty. I'll send you the coordinates. There will be Autobots and NEST commandos guarding the convoy's payload."

"What's the payload?" Clay asked.

"Ancient and very delicate Cybertronian technology," Douglas said. "But it's vital to our plans. Do not fail me, Stealth One."

"I won't!" Clay squeaked.

"I hope not," Douglas said, "for your sake. Stealth Leader out." He broke the connection.

Inside NEST headquarters, Kevin watched the technicians who had swarmed into Chief Lindsay's lab. Several were measuring the cubes that held the two Cybertronian cylinders while one shouted for someone to bring a forklift. Kittridge was trying to talk to at least five people at once, telling them what needed to be done to move the pillars safely, but he sounded increasingly flustered. Chief Lindsay, standing apart from the chaos with a quartet of armed soldiers, looked anxious.

The lab's double doors opened, admitting an industrial forklift with a flashing yellow light atop the cab. Kevin looked away from the forklift and faced Gears. “I wish there were some way to stop them,” he said. “If I were as strong as you, there’s no way I’d let them get away with this.” He returned his attention to the men and the forklift.

Gears peered curiously at Kevin. “Many of these so-called ‘expressions’ in your language confuse me,” Gears said. “But I believe I am beginning to understand some of them.”

Kevin looked back at Gears and said, “What are you talking about?”

“I said, ‘many of these so-called “expressions”—’ ”

“No, I heard what you said,” Kevin interrupted. “I just don’t know what you meant. What expression? Which one?”

“ ‘I won’t let them get away with this,’ ” Gears said proudly. Stepping away from Kevin, he tramped over to Lindsay and the soldiers. Lindsay looked up at Gears. Gears said, “Chief

Lindsay, Kevin and I understand that orders are orders. If General Marcus says the cylinder moves out tonight, that is what will happen."

Lindsay smiled with obvious relief. "I'm glad you two understand," the science officer said. "I promise you our work here is as important to me as it is to—"

Gears raised one hand to silence Lindsay. "But where the pillar goes," Gears said, "Kevin and I go, too."

Lindsay shrank back from Gears. "But... those aren't General Marcus's orders."

A stern-looking NEST lieutenant took a step toward Gears, but his resolve cracked when Gears directed his gaze back at him. The lieutenant moved aside as the Autobot stepped in front of the double doors, blocking the forklift's path.

The soldiers exchanged worried glances.

Kevin, seeing a potentially big problem developing, walked over to Chief Lindsay, tugged at the sleeve of his lab coat, and said, "Did General Marcus give any orders that we *couldn't* go?"

"No," Lindsay said.

"Then you're not disobeying him, are you?"

Lindsay looked to the NEST lieutenant. He shook his head. Lindsay looked back at Kevin and said, "Why do I get the feeling it would be impossible to stop the two of you from accompanying the truck?"

Kevin grinned.

"Very well, Kevin," Lindsay said. "I know how much this means to you. And if it's a safe enough operation for me, it ought to be safe enough for you."

"And me too," Gears added.

The NEST lieutenant leaned close to Lindsay

and said, "This isn't exactly proper protocol, Chief."

Lindsay replied, "Both Kevin Bowman and Gears have been very helpful with the scientific aspects of this project, and science decisions are *my* department. I'll take full responsibility." Stepping away from the lieutenant, Lindsay went beside Kevin and whispered, "But you and Gears will do exactly as I tell you. Agreed?"

"Of course, Chief," Kevin said.

Lindsay looked up at Gears and added, "I'm really sticking my neck out for you two."

"Really?" Gears trained his eyes on Lindsay's neck, and then said, "Your head does not appear to have extended any farther from your shoulders."

Lindsay sighed. "If I get court-martialed for not leaving you here and wind up in a military prison, maybe I'll finally get some rest!"

As Lindsay walked off to talk with Kittridge, Kevin said, "Gears, just so you know, 'sticking your neck out' is another expression. It means—"

"I know what it means, Kevin," Gears said. "I was just making a joke."

Kevin raised his eyebrows. "A joke? You made a joke?"

Gears nodded with pride. "I'm learning. And don't worry about Chief Lindsay. I won't let him get away with this. Or go to prison."

Kevin grinned. "I'm sure he'll appreciate that."

Chapter Nine

OFFENSE AND DEFENSE

Optimus Prime couldn't see the two robotic centipedes he was chasing, but with his audio sensors dialed up to maximum sensitivity, he could hear them. They made mechanical skittering noises as they moved through the forest. Optimus could hear those noises as clearly as the faint burble that rippled from the nearby river, the distant *thwock-thwock-thwock* of the NEST copter, and several hundred other noises his sensory algorithms had filtered out as unimportant at the moment.

Optimus wondered if any of his Autobot ancestors had ever encountered or heard about mechanicals like the centipedes and if they were even Cybertronian. As he searched his memories and sifted through enormous amounts of data, he found no references to them. All he knew for certain was what he had learned from his encounter with the creatures. They were very strong and extremely violent. And if they tried to harm any humans or other helpless life-forms on Earth, he would do everything he could to stop them.

Optimus froze. The noises he had heard ahead of him had gone silent. He realized the centipedes had stopped moving.

Centuries of instinct told Optimus to duck. The first centipede launched itself from the upper limbs of a pine tree where it had concealed itself. The creature's barbed-metal stinger whipped through the space where Optimus's head had been a split second earlier. Optimus spun and fired his cannons at the centipede, sending it tumbling through the air. Then he whirled in the other direction, just in time to catch the other one as it lurched out from behind another tree. The second centipede tried to close its jaws on the critical linkages below Optimus's jaw. Optimus held it at arm's length, and its electric stinger hammered against his chest armor. He could not help noticing several of the centipede's legs ended in melted stumps, damage he knew Ironhide had done.

Optimus's sensors detected an electric charge and realized the centipede in his grip was energizing its tail. Still clutching it, he turned fast to confront the other creature, which had landed in a tangle of brush. The centipede leaped from the brush, its jaws open in an apparent threat display. Optimus threw his arms forward and hurled the one from his chest into its ally. The thrown centipede's stinger discharged in a brilliant blue arc of electricity as the two collided midair.

The centipedes rolled in a tangle of fused metal, their segmented bodies spasming as currents shot through their limbs. One tore away from the other and wobbled up onto its damaged legs, right in front of Optimus's barrage cannon.

Optimus fired. The impact of the blast sent mechanical legs flying in all directions, and the centipede's eyeless head spun through the air before it landed with a thud at Optimus's feet. The head's jaws clattered angrily twice, then went still.

The other centipede rolled between a tight cluster of trees and vanished from Optimus's optical sensors. Optimus took a careful step forward. He scanned the area, and then took several more steps.

Moving past the trees, Optimus detected a faint smell of ozone. Looking ahead, he noticed a pile of leaves near a stand of young birches. Because of the position of branches overhead and how other leaves lay scattered around the pile, Optimus doubted that the pile had been formed naturally.

Suspicious, Optimus stooped and picked up a large dead branch that lay on the ground. He flung the branch ahead of him, into the mound of leaves.

The leaves exploded into flames. Optimus leaped forward as the centipede flung itself out from under the burning leaves. It moved with ferocious speed, driving its stinger into the gap between Optimus's chest plates as it whipped its jaws around to bite him. Optimus braced himself for a jolt of electricity from the centipede's tail and rapidly shifted his grip, moving his hands between the creature's head and its first pair of legs.

Optimus squeezed. Pistons squealed in his shoulders and back. His attacker's stinger thrashed beneath his chest plate. He could smell ozone again and sensed a gathering charge. He flexed his arms, breaking the creature's body in half.

Sparks erupted from the centipede's jaws and exposed midsection, and then its body went limp. Optimus jerked the stinger out of his abdomen and flung the broken monster to the ground.

The Autobot surveyed the wreckage. He considered gathering up parts from one of the lifeless creatures so that he could have them analyzed at NEST headquarters, but decided against it. He knew Ironhide and Ratchet might need his help, so he walked away from the wreckage and headed off to find his allies.

As Optimus moved through the forest, his thoughts strayed to Reverb. The Autobots had last seen the Decepticon in the form of a black jeep, fleeing the site of the ancient Cybertronian storehouse at Battle Mountain. Optimus wondered if Reverb or any other Decepticons were somehow connected with the robotic centipedes, or responsible for bringing them to Earth, or if the centipedes had their own invasion plan. He hoped he would learn the answer soon, before the arrival of any more dangerous meteoroids.

Move to the left, Reverb thought as he kept his eyes on the twelve Hyperdynamix tanks that were with him in the large cavern. The robot tanks moved, obeying his mental command. Then he instructed the rearmost tank to turn and raise its cannons, and he thought, *Fire!*

The rearmost tank spun and blasted the cavern wall, sending great chunks of rocks tumbling to the ground. Reverb grinned.

Once part of an abandoned mine, the cavern had been expanded as a hideout for the mysterious Stealth Leader and his minions. Reverb thought the tanks had performed well, the way they obeyed his silent commands instantly and went through their maneuvers in perfect formation. Being human-engineered technology, the tanks were primitive compared with Cybertronian machines, but they were powerful enough for Stealth Leader's purposes, and Reverb enjoyed making them an extension of his mechanical will.

But then an unwelcome voice sounded from a loudspeaker in the cavern. "Reverb? Reverb, may I have your attention?"

Reverb recognized Simon Clay's voice and said, "I'm busy."

"But... it's important."

"It better be!"

"The boss wants to talk to you," Clay said. "That important enough for you?"

Reverb growled. He disliked most of the disgusting little creatures on Earth. He considered humans as little more than pesky insects. The thought of crushing them made Reverb's logic circuits light up with anticipation. He could hardly wait for the day when Megatron ruled Earth, for then he would take great pleasure in wiping out all the insects, and he would make sure Simon Clay was among the first to die.

Until that day, Reverb would have to tolerate the pale, arrogant human, with his shifty eyes, just as he had to tolerate Simon Clay's "boss," Stealth Leader. Reverb hated to admit that Stealth Leader had resources and equipment and connections that he needed, but he hoped to eventually crush him, too.

From the loudspeaker, Simon Clay's voice boomed, "Reverb, did you hear me? The boss wants—"

"I heard you!" Reverb snapped.

"You don't have to yell," squeaked another voice from beside Reverb's head.

Reverb had forgotten about the tiny silver robot that was riding on his shoulder. He turned his head and magnified his view of the man-made robot.

"It's a shame you and Mr. Clay can't play nice," it continued, "especially since we're all on the same team. And why do you look so angry at me? I helped you escape from the NEST base, remember?"

"Shut up, Loudmouth," Reverb said.

"I keep tellin' ya, I don't like that name," the robot complained. "They got gratitude on your planet?"

Loudmouth had indeed used a surprisingly powerful stun weapon to rescue Reverb from captivity at the NEST base, but Reverb did not feel in any way indebted to the inferior robot, who insisted on staying close to him. Reverb ignored Loudmouth and silently sent an encrypted transmission to the tanks, ordering them to cease operations and hold their positions. He noted with approval that all twelve immediately stopped moving, then he turned and marched up the broad ramp that led out of the cavern. As he walked, the thick metal sliding door at the top of the ramp shot open.

Simon Clay had been standing on the other side, and he took several quick steps backward, eyes wide with fear at the sight of Reverb. The Decepticon did not slow his stride, forcing Clay to scramble aside as he cast an uneasy glance at the deadly sonic cannon that projected out of Reverb's chest armor.

"I'd appreciate it if you put your cannon away," Clay said.

Reverb stepped closer and lowered his glowing

eyes to the human's sweating face. "If I wanted to kill you, Clay," Reverb hissed, "I wouldn't need this weapon. All I'd need is the bottom of my foot."

Loudmouth chirped, "Boss is on the line!"

"Th-that's right," Clay stammered. "He—he wants you in the control center."

Reverb rose, muttering in annoyance as he turned and headed toward a long corridor. He was aware that Clay was trying to keep up with him, so he walked faster. When he reached the room filled with electronics designed for secure communications, Clay's footsteps were still echoing behind him. He came to a stop in front of the primary communications console.

"Is that you, Reverb?" asked Stealth Leader, his voice distorted by electronic filters as always.

"Yes," Reverb said tersely.

"Where's Clay?"

"Scuttling along somewhere."

"I'm here!" Clay gasped as he ran into the room.

"Good," Stealth Leader said. "The NEST convoy looks like it will be moving out with the Cybertronian cylinders in a couple hours, so accelerate your preparations. I'm sending you maps of the ambush site and surrounding areas now. Do you have them?"

Clay consulted a monitor, saw the maps appear on the screen, noted that the maps were for a nearby area of Nevada, and said, "Got 'em, boss."

Reverb grunted. He had already downloaded the same maps, converted them to three-dimensional forms, overlaid them with satellite photographs and tourist snapshots uploaded to social networks, and begun to analyze three potential ambush tactics.

Stealth Leader said, "Do you have the maps, Reverb?"

"Yes," Reverb said.

"And do you understand the plan?"

Reverb snorted. "I was ambushing my enemies when your kind was bashing beasts over the heads with stones."

"Oooh," said Loudmouth.

"Good to know," Stealth Leader said. "I'm glad you've had thousands of years to learn to follow directions."

Loudmouth chuckled. Reverb allowed himself a brief vivid fantasy of flicking the little robot across the room, and then using his weapons to reduce Loudmouth to a silver puddle.

Reverb said, "Tell me, Stealth Leader...will Optimus Prime be part of this NEST convoy?"

"Optimus Prime is elsewhere," Stealth Leader said, "but Gears and Bumblebee will be."

Reverb hissed so hard that steam erupted from the sides of his neck, causing Loudmouth to duck away from the blast. "Gears has caused me a bunch of pain. I'm gonna enjoy pulling him apart, piece by piece," he said.

"Before you pull anyone apart," Stealth Leader continued, "I've also learned that Kevin Bowman—the boy from Hurley's Crossing—will also be with the convoy."

"Bowman?!" Reverb released another blast of steam. He remembered Bowman as the insect who saved Gears from the death he so richly deserved and who had helped the Autobot during the fight at Hawthorne. "If it weren't for that kid," Reverb fumed, "I wouldn't have been captured by NEST."

Loudmouth chirped, "But if you hadn't been captured, I wouldn't have had the pleasure of rescuing you! Aren't you glad we met?"

"Shut up, Loudmouth," Reverb said. "Just... shut... up!"

Stealth Leader said, "Listen carefully, Reverb. If you encounter Kevin Bowman, do not harm him."

"Why not?" demanded Reverb. "The brat certainly deserves it. What possible importance can he have?"

"That's none of your business," Stealth Leader said. "Your job is to fulfill your mission objectives. Can you handle that?"

"But what if Bowman gets in the way of my objectives?" Reverb asked. "What then? Do you expect me to just say, 'Keep the Cybertronian cylinders, kid! This one's on me.' Would that make you happy?" Not bothering to conceal the contempt in his voice, Reverb added, "Tell me, *boss*, just how much do you want the cylinders?"

Stealth Leader was silent for a moment, and then said, "I want the cylinders, and I want them undamaged. Do what has to be done."

"So, you're saying Bowman is expendable?"

"I'm saying I have reason for the boy to remain unharmed, but acquiring the cylinders is more important."

"And how about Gears? You're sure you won't lose sleep if I destroy him?"

"Reverb," Stealth Leader said, "I never lose sleep. That's because I—unlike you—know how to get a job done right the first time.

Now move out." Stealth Leader broke the connection.

Reverb growled in irritation and clenched his metal hands into fists. He didn't like working for insects, or putting up with their insults. He muttered, "If I don't crush somebody soon, I'll go nuts."

"Excuse me," Clay said as he darted out of the communications room and ran back up the corridor.

"Oh, boy!" Loudmouth squealed. "I have a feeling somebody's really gonna get it today!"

"Funny," Reverb said. "I was thinking the same thing." He plucked Loudmouth from his shoulder, wrapped his fingers tightly around the small robot, and then squeezed. Loudmouth emitted a single electronic yelp as Reverb squashed the robot's body into compact bits. Opening his hand to examine Loudmouth's remains, Reverb added, "And I'm just getting started."

"Move yer pistons, Ratchet!" Ironhide yelled. "We gotta get between these robo-pedes and that town!"

"Robo-pedes?" Ratchet yelled back. "That's your name for our opponents?"

"Yup!" Ironhide said with glee. "What else are you gonna call robotic centipedes?"

The two Autobots rushed down the forested hill, chasing their targets. Emerging from the woods, Ironhide and Ratchet ran through a field and spotted the creatures a hundred feet ahead of them. The centipedes skittered quickly across a two-lane highway. The Autobots followed.

"The river is directly ahead," Ratchet said to Ironhide.

"Run faster!" Ironhide said. "We have to stop them!"

The Autobots ran down a slope and spotted the two creatures heading straight for the river. The centipedes continued running until their front legs hit the water; they slammed to a halt, lifting their heads and waving their legs in confusion.

"They can't swim!" Ratchet said.

"I'm not waiting for them to rust to death," Ironhide said as he raised one arm. Before Ratchet could object, Ironhide fired a missile that went screaming toward the centipedes. It plowed into the ground between the two creatures, sending pieces of legs flying. They crumpled and tumbled onto their backs by the river's edge.

"Direct hit!" Ironhide crowed.

"Not quite," Ratchet observed as the centipedes rolled their segmented bodies and heaved themselves into the water, their remaining legs churning like propellers. They shot across the river, leaving two wakes of white water behind them.

"Looks like you're wrong," Ironhide said. "They *can* swim."

Ratchet said, "You certainly encouraged them to try."

"Did not," said Ironhide. The two Autobots stomped into the river, which quickly became deep enough that they had to advance with ungainly splashing leaps. As they proceeded after their targets, Ironhide added, "I know you didn't approve of me firing that missile, but you've got to admit, by destroying a few of their legs, I probably slowed them down a bit."

Ratchet activated several auxiliary logic circuits and checked the map of the area. "I'm afraid you didn't slow them down enough," he said. "They're still moving so fast that they'll reach the town before we do. But there's a road on the shore to the right, and I think if we assume vehiclular form, we can beat them."

"Then let's do it!" Ironhide said.

They cut right, leaped up onto the shore, and ran until they reached the road. As they ran, both Autobots began to change their bodies. Within seconds, Ironhide had reconfigured his into a black pickup truck; Ratchet was a military rescue vehicle. The two then took off with a squeal of tires, leaving black streaks of smoking rubber on the asphalt.

"Be careful!" Ratchet shouted as Ironhide wrapped around a curve. "Humans might be traveling this road!"

"I am being careful!" Ironhide replied as he accelerated. Seconds later, they arrived at the edge of town, ahead of the centipedes. The Autobots rapidly returned to their bipedal forms. They rushed into the woods, their sensors dialed to maximum sensitivity.

"I hear something," Ironhide said, and then Ratchet heard the noise, too: a faint *scritch-scritch-scritch* approaching them. The Autobots tracked the noise and used their other sensors to confirm they were the only things between the town and the approaching centipedes. They stood still and silent, waiting.

Ratchet heard something move beneath the trees to his right. He turned to see a brown deer with white spots, its tail flipping as it sniffed the air.

Ironhide saw the deer, too. "You're thinkin' that's pretty," he whispered to Ratchet, "but remember what Optimus said. We're not here for sightseeing."

"I know," Ratchet said. "But...it's just so beautiful."

The deer looked at Ratchet, then turned unexpectedly from the Autobots' position and leaped away, skipping toward a clearing before a stand of trees. Ratchet realized the deer was headed straight for the two centipedes.

And then the creatures showed themselves. Still dripping with water, they emerged from the stand of trees just beyond the deer, who now stood in their path, frozen with terror. They made clacking noises as they moved into the clearing.

Ironhide and Ratchet realized that the eyeless centipedes did not notice the deer. The Autobots stood still. Ratchet kept his eyes on the deer and silently pleaded for the animal to run to safety.

The deer remained motionless for two agonizingly long seconds, then turned and raced through the grass. The centipedes rumbled straight ahead, paying no attention to the fleeing animal. Then the deer snapped a twig in its path. The centipedes' monstrous heads came up, turned to face the noise, then shifted back before the creatures resumed their journey toward the town.

The robo-pedes are blind, Ratchet thought. He turned to Ironhide and silently pointed to his eyes with his good hand. Ironhide understood, and responded with a nod.

The Autobots remained silent as the centipedes churned ahead, branches snapping under their metal bodies. Both Ratchet and Ironhide noticed how they did not bother to avoid the trees in their path, but instead struck the trees with their heads and then kept going. Despite their somewhat meandering course, the centipedes were heading straight for the Autobots.

Ironhide's arms quietly rearranged themselves into cannons. Ratchet changed his hand into a saw. Ironhide calculated the distance to the creatures. *Thirty feet away... twenty feet... ten...*

He fired his cannons at point-blank range at the nearest centipede. The featureless metal head exploded into splinters and the body began to jerk in spasmodic twists.

Ratchet activated his saw with a scream of metal and leaped at the second one, lowering his shoulder to ram it into the creature's jaw. He swung at its neck, hoping to sever its head from the rest of its body. The saw connected, sending bits of metal flying. The centipede screeched and pushed past Ratchet. He tried to grab it, but his other arm hung uselessly by his side. It flung its stinger sideways, and Ratchet ducked. His saw bit into the ground, sending streams of black dirt skyward.

"Ironhide!" Ratchet yelled as the creature rushed off into the forest.

Ironhide turned from inspecting the fallen centipede and saw what had happened. "Aw, no you don't!" he yelled as he clomped off in pursuit, his pulse cannons barking fire.

The centipede turned away from the town and moved as fast as it could for a cluster of trees that ringed the shore of a deep, blue lake. Heavy branches cracked and splintered as the creature shoved its way through. Ironhide was just several yards behind when it arrived at the shoreline.

Five fishermen in plaid shirts and waders looked up in horror as the giant metal centipede raced past them and flung itself into the water, followed by a massive black robot with cannons for arms.

"Looks like I'm goin' fishin', too!" Ironhide said as he dived into the lake.

The waters roiled as the centipede's tail thrashed back and forth, slapping at the surface. A loud explosion sent a blast of water all the way back to the shore. The area was still bubbling as a scarred black head emerged from the lake, followed by broad shoulders and thick arms.

Ironhide waded back to the shore. Under one arm, he held a length of the centipede's neck and most of its head; under his other arm, he carried two of the creature's legs. He flung the parts onto the ground as he came to a stop a short distance from the humans, who stared at him with awe.

Ironhide looked from the fishermen to what was left of his opponent. Then he looked back at the fishermen and said, "Did you see it?" He spread his arms as wide as they would go. "With the tail still on, that sucker was *this big*!"

Chapter Ten
MIGHTY CONVOY

Military convoys weren't an uncommon sight on the lonely roads of southwestern Nevada, so few civilian drivers were surprised when police told them they would have to wait for one to pass. Jeeps and armored trucks led the NEST group. Three identical eighteen-wheelers and another line of armored trucks followed. A yellow-and-black sports car with dark tinted windows was distracting enough to draw civilians' attention away from the more unusual sight of the armored truck directly behind the last of the eighteen-wheelers. It had no one behind the wheel, but a boy was in the passenger seat.

Kevin Bowman patted the truck's dashboard and said, "How are you feeling, Gears?"

"Fine, thank you," Gears's voice rumbled from the radio. "Do you think I'm blending in well with the other vehicles?"

"You look great. Definitely blending in. And you definitely look better than you used to. No reason you had to keep looking like an SUV that had been on blocks for years."

Gears was silent for several seconds, then said, "I suspect you'd have preferred riding with a more comfortable car, perhaps like Bumblebee."

"Nothing against him," Kevin said, "but I'm glad to ride with you. We make a good team.

But now that you mention him, how's Bumblebee doing?"

"I will ask him," Gears said. He transmitted a short-range communications burst to Bumblebee, whose vocal processor had been damaged years ago. Bumblebee had stubbornly resisted the best efforts of Autobots and humans to fix his processor—as he had come to prefer communicating by way of popular music.

Kevin said, "Well?"

Gears said, "I did not recognize the song Bumblebee shared, but I believe he is . . . enthusiastic."

"I'm glad he's happy," Kevin said with a smile, but the smile faded as he stared out into the deepening gloom.

"Is something wrong, Kevin?" Gears said. "Chief Lindsay *did* allow us to accompany the convoy and protect the cylinders."

"I know," Kevin said. "But I'm so scared about Duane that I can barely think straight. And...I guess I don't know how to say this."

"Say what?"

"Gears, why are you here?"

Gears was quiet for a moment, then said, "It is my duty. I was sent here to prevent Reverb from seizing the contents of the munitions stronghold established by ancient Cybertronians. That content includes the cylinders, as you call them. As I told Chief Lindsay, I cannot let those cylinders out of my sight if I believe they are in jeopardy."

"I understand," Kevin said.

"I'm not finished, Kevin. Although your brother's safety is not part of my mission, I will do everything I can to see that he returns to you safely."

"Thank you, Gears."

"You are welcome. Does my answer improve your emotional well-being?"

Kevin smiled. "You sure have a funny way of putting things."

"Really?" Gears said. "I was not trying to be funny."

Kevin smiled sadly. "Life has been so crazy since... well, since I first met you. It's like... I used to be just a *kid*, trying to help out my brother and get a good grade on my science homework. And now my house is empty, guarded by soldiers, and I haven't seen my friends in weeks and I live at an Army base and instead of worrying whether it's too dark to ride my bike over to my friend Gilbert Poole's house, I'm worrying if an alien machine is going to activate and drag everything nearby halfway across the universe. It feels like I'm dreaming, but... I can't wake up."

"We are at war, Kevin," Gears said. "It is a hard life. There is always the possibility that you will fall in battle, that your Spark will be extinguished. There is also the fear that you will forget what life was like before and discover that war has become the only thing you understand. I have seen it happen to Cybertronians before. It is a terrible thing."

Kevin nodded. "So what do your people do to keep that from happening?"

"There is no simple answer. But we try to remember why we fight. We fight to protect the innocent, so that they may know peace. And we try to help our friends."

The sun was sinking behind the mountains in the west. Looking at the sunset and the clouds streaked with red and gold, Kevin felt tears welling up in his eyes.

"I have been at war for many years, Kevin,"

Gears said. "I have lost many friends, and I grieve for them. But I have gained friends, too. Friends like you, Kevin. And that is a good thing, despite so much that is bad."

Kevin wiped away his tears. "I'm glad we're friends, too, Gears."

"Is your emotional well-being improved now?" Gears asked.

Kevin laughed. "Yes, Gears," he said. "Yes, really, I do feel a little better. Thanks."

Reverb had to admit Stealth Leader had chosen a good spot for an ambush. The Decepticon was with Simon Clay on a ridge south of the little town of Beatty. The ridge offered a good view of the area below, where Highway 99 passed through a gap in the rocky hills.

Simon Clay had hidden his black surveillance van behind a low hill to the west, and was now lying atop the ridge, peering at the highway through expensive night-vision binoculars. Reverb stood beside him, silhouetted against the sky and making no effort to hide.

"You don't need those," Reverb said, gesturing to the binoculars. "You'll see the trucks' headlights soon enough."

Clay said, "There might be an advance team."

"They're not expecting trouble," Reverb said. "Military payloads go up and down this road every week. They'll never know what hit them."

Clay said, "I want to be sure there isn't an advance team." He continued scanning the hills to the south. "What are those lights over there, about three miles away?"

Reverb glanced in the direction Clay was pointing, and then said, "That's Hyperdynamix Aerospace."

"Hyperdynamix?" Clay said, alarmed. "They made the tanks! The tanks we stole from their own facility!"

"Different division," said Reverb dismissively. "That was Hyperdynamix Laboratories in Mission City, nowhere near here. Hyperdynamix Aerospace is a military contractor, more concerned about their project than anything happening in the outside world."

Clay put down his binoculars. "I suppose you're right. And now that I think of it, if Stealth Leader had been worried about the proximity of the Hyperdynamix facility to our position, he would have said something."

"Quiet!" Reverb said. "I can hear the convoy. I estimate it's about a mile away."

Clay said, "I don't hear anything."

"Your kind never does," Reverb said. "Compared to an advanced life-form like me, you're essentially as deaf as a rock."

"Maybe I should wait in my van."

"Why, so you can drive off into the night if things go wrong?"

"No, of course not," Clay protested feebly. "Are the tanks in position?"

"Of course," Reverb said. "Four on each ridge, then four more in reserve. We'll block the road with four, send in two from each side, and then cut off the convoy's rear with the last four."

Clay said, "And then what?"

Reverb said, "And then we'll take the Cybertronian cylinders and destroy the entire convoy."

Chapter Eleven
HIGHWAY BATTLE

Kevin and Gears were halfway through a game of Twenty Questions when the taillights of the eighteen-wheeler ahead of them turned red, and the truck slammed to a sudden stop.

Kevin said, "Why are we stopping here?"

"I am not certain," Gears replied. A moment later, a burst of static emitted from the radio followed by a musical warning from Bumblebee, informing his friends there was danger and heartbreak ahead.

Kevin said, "Danger?!"

And just then a missile slammed into the ground ahead causing a huge explosion. Dirt and stones began to rain down on the trucks and armored vehicles.

"We're under attack!" Kevin said, fumbling blindly to release his seat belt.

"Kevin!" Gears called out. "Stay in your seat!"

But Kevin's ears were ringing as he stumbled out of the passenger door, twisting his ankle.

NEST commandos, with their guns at the ready, leaped out of the vehicles in front of Kevin. He rubbed his eyes and blinked, struggling to regain his vision. Stepping away from Gears, he continued blinking as he turned to see approaching commandos. Their night-vision goggles made them look like bug-eyed creatures from another world.

"What's going on?" Kevin shouted.

"Attackers ahead of us!" a NEST commando yelled back. "Get down, kid! We'll handle this!"

Kevin saw a cluster of large yellow sheets of metal rise away from the convoy, and he realized he was looking at Bumblebee changing forms. Bumblebee was still locking his arms and legs into place when Kevin heard a whirring noise beside him and turned to see tires and car parts retracting into Gears's chassis. Gears extended his own arms and legs, rose to his full height, and said, "Stay here, Kevin. I will help Bumblebee."

"I'll go with you!"

"No, Kevin." Gears's blue eyes glowed bright in the darkness. "We are in danger, and you will only be in harm's way. Stay under cover."

Kevin nodded and Gears tromped off down

the highway, limping slightly. Kevin saw a rapid flash of impacts up ahead and felt waves of pressure from the explosions a split second later. He heard machine-gun fire and men yelling orders. More missiles soared overhead. He scrambled behind the military vehicle, a personnel carrier that had come to a stop behind the spot where Gears had changed into his bipedal form. Kevin ducked down with his hands covering his head, his mind reeling, trying to make sense of the chaos all around him.

Another missile detonated. And then Kevin was lying in the road, shielding his face against a wave of heat that had already singed his hair and eyebrows. He couldn't hear anything. He blinked and saw that the personnel carrier he'd been hiding behind was now in flames, lying upside down and sideways across the road as if a giant hand had flipped it over.

Kevin scrambled to his knees and saw flashes in the darkness on both sides of the highway. A group of NEST commandos raced off the road and knelt down, firing wildly into the night.

On the other side of the road, yet another exploding missile momentarily turned the night into day and showed Kevin a vision from his nightmares. Two dull black shapes were descending the hill on treads. Turrets extended from their bodies, ending in long gun barrels. The turrets fired, each launching a missile through the air. The explosives struck an eighteen-wheeler and instantly turned it into a massive ball of fire.

Those aren't Decepticons, Kevin thought. He realized the attacking vehicles were robot tanks, the same tanks that had been reported stolen from Hyperdynamix Laboratories while he, Gears, and Douglas had been exploring the secrets of Battle Mountain.

Kevin turned to warn the NEST commandos, but another fireball lit up the sky. Two more tanks were coming from the other direction.

This is bad, Kevin thought. *This is very bad.*

Gears had told him to stay under cover, but sticking close to the personnel carrier had nearly gotten him killed. He suspected Gears and Bumblebee were busy with whatever was attacking them from the front and wondered if they might have any idea of the threats closing in from the sides. His instincts told him he had to warn them.

Kevin got to his feet and ducked behind the rear wheels of the last of the three trucks, the one that carried the Cybertronian cylinders.

He peeked around the wheels to see if the way was clear, then he jerked his head back in horror.

A tall figure was striding down the hillside to the west, the flames and flashes of the battle reflected in the robot's chrome body. A massive cone extended from his chest.

Reverb.

Kevin ran back the way he'd come, screaming and waving his arms in an effort to get the soldiers' attention. "Look out!" he yelled, but he could barely hear himself. "Reverb's coming!"

Alarms sounded at Hyperdynamix Aerospace. In the secure conference room, Dr. Porter and General Marcus exchanged startled looks. Porter jabbed irritably at his keyboard.

"Command post," Porter said. "What's happening out there?"

Lyons, the mission controller, responded, "Perimeter security reports an attack three miles north on Highway Ninety-Nine, Dr. Porter. Observation drones are on their way."

"The convoy," Marcus said as he rose from his chair.

Porter looked at Marcus. "Convoy? What convoy?"

But Marcus wasn't listening. He had pulled out his secure phone and was barking into it, trying to find out what was happening. Porter returned his attention to his own computer and said, "Put the feed from the drones' cameras on the big screen."

The monitor winked on, and Porter and Marcus saw an aerial view of a raging battle, transmitted directly from a flying drone. Tinted green by the drone's night-vision optics, the monitor displayed burning military vehicles surrounded by soldiers who were scrambling to take up defensive positions. Two Autobots, their pulse cannons blazing, were trying to protect the humans. Then Porter and Marcus sighted enemy forces.

"No," Porter muttered. "It can't be. Those are my tanks...my property!" He pulled open a drawer in the conference room table, extracted a silver joystick, and tapped his computer. "Lyons! Give me control of the lead drone!"

"Relinquishing control, Doctor," Lyons replied.

Porter adjusted the joystick until he had the drone's camera aimed at one of the dark shapes attacking the convoy. Marcus pointed to the big screen and said, "Look there! That's not one of your tanks. That's—"

"Reverb," both men said at the same time. Porter zeroed in on the tall figure with the cone in its chest. Porter said, "The tanks are creating a diversion intended to draw out our defenses. The Decepticon's real target is Hyperdynamix Aerospace. Reverb stole my tanks, and now he wants my satellite."

Reverb stopped, his blazing eyes staring directly at the airborne camera. He raised his arm and a flash of light filled the screen, followed by static.

Marcus said, "I really don't think you're the target, Doctor."

"Then what is?" Porter demanded. "What's your convoy carrying?"

"That's classified."

Porter shook his head in disgust and stabbed at his communicator. "Prepare to launch the RLVs. I want liftoff for RLV-2 in twenty minutes and RLV-3 three minutes after that."

"Dr. Porter," Marcus interjected. "I must object to this hasty and ill-advised decision."

"Your objection is noted, General. And rejected. The war with the Decepticons ends tonight!"

Chapter Twelve
OUTNUMBERED!

Bumblebee and Gears stood side by side, their plasma cannons blasting at two approaching enemy robot tanks. Behind the Autobots, the NEST commandos fired machine guns at the same targets. Bullets pinged off the tanks without causing any obvious damage.

Glancing at Bumblebee, Gears said, "Ironhide fought these tanks in a training exercise. They were tough even for him. We should direct our attack on one robot at a time."

Bumblebee broadcast a flourish of oldies to announce "*It takes two*," which Gears decided was an agreement.

Turning to the NEST commandos, Gears said, "Concentrate your fire on the tank to the right." As the commandos complied, Gears and Bumblebee sprinted toward the tank to their left. The tank fired bullets directly at the Autobots, but the bullets bounced off their armored chests. The Autobots were still running toward the tank when it raised itself up on its rear treads and launched a missile, forcing Bumblebee and Gears to duck.

The missile whizzed over Gears's back and smashed into a fallen tree. Gears and Bumblebee got to their feet and sprang toward the tank. The yellow Autobot leaped and landed atop the tank's turret while Gears tackled the tank's tread-equipped legs. The tank jerked back and forth, trying to dislodge Bumblebee.

"Hold on!" Gears said. The tank extended a flamethrower and blasted fire across his arm. As Gears's sensors shrieked, he jammed his fist under the tank's turret, where it met the machine's body. Gears's forearm pistons whined as his arm turned into a cannon.

"Jump!" he shouted. Bumblebee leaped away from the robot tank and was still in midair when Gears fired. The power of the blast drove Gears backward and he landed in the dust. Rolling onto his side, he looked up and saw the tank sitting in front of him, smoke pouring from the hole where its head used to be.

Just then, a massive explosion shook the atmosphere. The Autobots glanced back and saw that another eighteen-wheeler had burst into flames. Gears spotted a bulky silhouette move in front of the blazing truck.

"Reverb," Gears muttered. And then he shouted, "Kevin! Get down!"

Reverb heard Gears and swung his missile launcher in his direction. He had Gears in the crosshairs of his targeting scope when Kevin ran out from behind a truck and moved directly into the missile's projected flight path. Seeing the boy appear in the crosshairs, the Decepticon remembered Stealth Leader's orders.

Reverb ducked behind the nearest burning truck. He performed a quick survey of his tanks. One had been destroyed; four were still held in reserve, in case the NEST convoy tried to retreat the way it had come. That left seven at Reverb's immediate disposal, which he considered more than enough.

The Decepticon's mechanical mouth twisted

into a wicked grin as he sent three tanks to engage the Autobots and then directed the other four to attack the last eighteen-wheeler.

Douglas let out a sigh of relief as he watched the battle unfold on his notebook. He had done his best to keep Kevin Bowman alive, but he hadn't expected Kevin to start running around like an idiot *trying* to get killed by Reverb. He also hadn't been certain that Reverb would obey Stealth Leader's command not to harm Kevin, but evidently, Reverb was complying.

Everything will work out fine, Douglas thought. *Just as I planned*.

He glanced at the other windows open on his screen and studied the images being transmitted and recorded by his various spybots and intrusion programs. His attention was drawn toward one with a view inside a Hyperdynamix Aerospace control room. He enlarged the image to see his father and General Marcus shouting at each other.

Douglas rewound the video to nearly a full minute earlier, then pressed Play.

Douglas grimaced. He knew that if his father launched the satellite and brought an end to the war, he'd likely spend the rest of his life in his father's shadow, with no one ever knowing or caring about his own accomplishments. Douglas said, "Oh no you don't, Father."

"Gears!" Kevin screamed. "Bumblebee!" Heedless of the bullets zipping through the air, he ran to his Autobot allies.

Gears shouted, "Kevin! Stay down!" He fired another blast at a roving robot tank as Kevin raced up beside him.

"Reverb's here!" Kevin panted. "He's leading the tanks!"

"I know," Gears said. "I saw him, too. But you are in danger here. Seek shelter until the fight is over."

"But he'll get the Cybertronian cylinder!" Kevin said as Gears shoved him behind his own massive body. Bullets pinged and sparked across Gears's chest. Bumblebee moved fast to Kevin's other side, and more bullets ricocheted off the second Autobot's back.

Kevin peered past Gears's mechanical legs to see a trio of robot tanks moving toward them. "We are outnumbered. Kevin, I may not be able to protect you while fighting the tanks. Please, Kevin...run and hide," Gears said.

Kevin looked at his Cybertronian friend. His armor was covered with small pits and dents, and his joints were dripping lubricant. Kevin nodded, then turned and broke away, sprinting for the hills to the west.

Reverb walked toward the highway, preceded by the robot tanks, where the wrecked trucks and personnel carriers continued to burn. Bullets bounced off the Decepticon's shoulders and chest. He looked down at the humans and their primitive weapons.

"It's squashing time!" Reverb said as he fired his sonic cannon, releasing a pulse of crushing sound that knocked the soldiers backward. Moving closer to the road, Reverb sent a silent command to his tanks: *"Destroy the truck."*

The tanks' turrets pointed at the last intact truck, then opened fire. Missiles streaked into its body, sending a flower of fire up into the night.

A voice buzzed inside Reverb's head. "Reverb, this is Stealth Leader."

Reverb thought Stealth Leader sounded more excited than usual, maybe even agitated. "What do you want now?" Reverb said. "I'm busy." He ignored the soldiers as he stepped onto the highway. The truck was burning, its trailer reduced to a blackened, twisted metal skeleton.

Stealth Leader said, "Hyperdynamix Aerospace is about to launch a satellite."

"How nice for them," Reverb said, kicking aside a blazing tire. "Why should I care about some insect science project?" Before Stealth Leader could respond, Reverb said, "Ah, there you are!" He'd seen the large glass cube holding the cylinder from Battle Mountain resting in the middle of the highway.

"Shut up and listen, Reverb! Porter has created a communications network in space. That satellite is the key to the network. If it's launched, it will send out a signal that can be received anywhere on Earth."

A couple of NEST commandos jumped in front of the cube and then fired their guns at Reverb. He sent them flying with a single swipe of one metal hand. He looked at the cube and saw that one side of it was partly cracked, but the cylinder within was undamaged. He examined the Cybertronian numbers that glowed on the cylinder's readouts.

"Reverb!" Stealth Leader's voice rang out inside Reverb's skull.

"What?!" Reverb shouted back. "What were you saying? Something about a satellite?"

"If the satellite launches," Stealth Leader said, "it will transmit a signal that will melt the logic circuits of every Decepticon on the planet."

Reverb stared blankly at the cylinder in the cracked cube. "Every Decepticon? That's impossible."

"Porter thinks it's possible," Stealth Leader said. "So does NEST. Do you want to risk your life on your enemies being wrong?"

Reverb shoved one hand through the cube's side, shattering the glass as he reached for the cylinder.

"Stop that launch, Reverb!" Stealth Leader said. "Do whatever you have to do."

Reverb looked around and pulled his hand

out of the cube, leaving the cylinder inside. He activated another communications channel and said, "Reverb to Stealth One. Change of plans. Take over the tanks."

"What?" Clay yelped from Reverb's built-in radio. "Why?"

"Because I have more important things to do than swat insects," Reverb said. He took one last look at the cylinder, then turned and ran down the highway, away from the battle and straight for the Hyperdynamix launch site.

Chapter Thirteen
DR. PORTER'S GIFT

The three robot tanks that had been firing at Bumblebee and Gears suddenly stopped and darted around the burning wreckage. Two of the tanks quickly took cover and resumed firing at the Autobots, distracting them while the third tank shifted stealthily behind.

"They're encircling us," Gears said to Bumblebee. "Assume defensive posture, back-to-back."

Bumblebee's speakers burbled with a short burst of punk rock that concluded they were stranded on their own. He moved up behind Gears so that they faced away from each other. The tanks moved closer and suddenly stopped.

One moved jerkily forward, then back, as if it was uncertain which way it wanted to go. Then it began to advance again, but it moved left, into the path of the tank next to it.

Gears realized something was wrong. He elbowed Bumblebee and yelled, "Go!" The two Autobots charged at the confused tank, their pulse cannons blazing. The tank fell back, opening and closing weapons hatches. Gears and Bumblebee fired missiles directly into the hatches, causing it to explode across the highway.

Gears looked at Bumblebee and said, "Why did the tank malfunction?" Bumblebee shrugged. Then Gears said, "The cylinder!"

The two Autobots raced toward the shattered glass cube.

In his van, Simon Clay scanned the twelve screens on his console. Ten showed the same view from one camera on a Hyperdynamix tank. Two were completely black and showed nothing.

Clay threw switches frantically, trying to remember which controls operated which weapons, while his eyes flicked back and forth among the ten working screens. Somehow managing to get another tank's camera to work, he saw a NEST commando carrying a shoulder-mounted antitank weapon aimed directly at the camera. Before he could figure out which tank was connected to that particular camera, or which control operated that particular tank, the screen was filled with a burst of bright white light, then immediately snapped to black.

Clay hammered his fists on the console in frustration. "Reverb!" he shouted. "This is all your fault!"

Inside Hyperdynamix Aerospace, General Marcus had excused himself to a small conference room. He activated his cell phone and called NEST headquarters. "This is Marcus!" he bellowed. "The Yucca Mountain convoy is under attack and that fool Porter is going to launch his untested satellite weapons! Where's Optimus Prime?"

A NEST controller answered, "Optimus Prime is aware of the situation, sir. He is presently inbound from the Idaho contact site with Ironhide and Ratchet. Estimated time of arrival is thirty minutes."

"That's not soon enough," Marcus said. "What NEST units were accompanying the convoy?"

The controller read off a list of commando units. Marcus frowned. The commandos were good soldiers, but the combination of Reverb and robot tanks was beyond anything they'd trained for. Marcus was still frowning when the controller added, "The convoy also included Bumblebee, Gears, Chief Lindsay..."

"Stop right there!" Marcus said. "*Which* Autobots did you say are out there?"

"Bumblebee and Gears, sir," the controller repeated.

"Blazing bombs!" Marcus yelled. "Why is Gears with them?"

"Sir, Chief Lindsay approved the—"

"Never mind," Marcus interrupted. "Patch me through to Gears. Now!"

Almost fifteen seconds passed before Marcus heard Gears say, "Yes, General Marcus?"

"Come to the Hyperdynamix launch complex immediately," Marcus said. "Dr. Porter is about to launch his killer satellite, and I have a bad feeling that he's not just planning to kill Decepticons!"

Douglas's jaw hung open. Three tanks had been destroyed, and camera views from the other tanks showed NEST commandos forming into fire teams, while the remaining tanks trundled back and forth awkwardly in the desert.

"Stealth Leader to Stealth One! What's going on?" asked Douglas.

Stammering with fear, Simon Clay replied, "Reverb's g-g-gone! I'm piloting the tanks, but the NEST teams are counterattacking, and—"

"Why are *you* piloting the tanks?" Douglas interrupted.

"Reverb ran off. He *left* me to operate the tanks! I've never piloted them before, and I don't know how to—"

"They're designed to run autonomously!" Douglas exploded. "They don't *need* you to drive them!"

Simon Clay was silent for a moment, then said, "But...I thought you reprogrammed them when Reverb—"

"I *did* reprogram them!" Douglas said. "But I didn't get rid of the old programming that enabled the robots to function on their own! Why would I do that?" Douglas put his head in his hands. He squeezed his eyes shut as he tried to contain his anger, then he blinked and returned his gaze to the computer screen. The screen's largest window showed his father screaming orders at terrified-looking technicians in a control room. Douglas scanned the others.

Reverb. Where's Reverb?

Struggling to remain calm, Douglas said, "How many tanks are left?"

"Nine," Clay replied. "Wait, make that eight. I-I found the settings for autonomous programming."

Douglas felt like hurling his laptop into a

wall. Instead, he said, "Switch the surviving tanks to autonomous programming and order a full retreat. Select targets of opportunity only. And get the tanks out of there!"

He slammed the screen down onto the keypad, picked up his cell phone, tapped two numbers to contact his pilot, and said, "Prepare the chopper. I want to be out of here in three minutes."

Kevin ran halfway up a slope of loose dirt before he turned to look down at the battle he'd left below. He spotted several robot tanks fleeing the burning convoy, and then Gears and Bumblebee. Gears appeared to be talking animatedly. Kevin wondered what Bumblebee was saying in response.

A dark shape shifted below Kevin's position. He gasped as it grew larger and he realized it was a tank trundling after him, its treads climbing the hill with ease.

Kevin scrambled to his right, hoping to get out of the tank's path, but his foot dislodged some small stones. As he struggled to regain his footing, the tank's turret spun in his direction.

The machine guns opened fire. Bullets smashed into the ground just a few feet away from Kevin. He scrambled higher up the slope, moving on an angular path. The tank followed, its treads whining.

Kevin jumped up, faced the Autobots in the distance, and yelled, "Help! Gears! Bumblebee!"

Bumblebee looked away from Gears, and for a moment, Kevin thought the Autobot had heard him. But Bumblebee turned and jogged down the highway toward the burned-out shells of the trucks, while Gears looked the other way, to the south.

The tank fired. Kevin dived onto his belly, his face smacking the dirt. The missile ripped through the hillside above, setting fire to a scraggly stand of bushes. Once clear, Kevin jumped to his feet and screamed as loudly as he could. "*Gears!*"

Kevin's voice echoed off the hills. He saw Gears stop and look around. Then Kevin saw the blue of the Autobot's eyes.

"See me," Kevin said as the tank readied another missile. "Please see me, Gears." Kevin saw the mighty Autobot run up the hill as fast as he could, bounding to accommodate his left leg, which dragged slightly behind him. Gears's missile blasted into the ground below the tank, causing it to teeter back on its treads. When he reached the tank, he seized it and grabbed its long gun barrel.

The tank extended a silver tube—a microwave emitter designed to destroy Cybertronian circuits—from its upper surface. Gears chopped at it, then yanked on the gun barrel with both hands. The tank's treads spun crazily, sending up a plume of gravel, before the vehicle fell and tumbled down the hillside. Gears ran after it, his big feet slipping and sliding. He rammed his arm against the tank and blasted it, shattering its frame. The tank exploded as Gears flipped away from the wreckage and landed on his feet.

Kevin scrambled down the hill to rejoin his friend. "I'm sorry, Gears! I ran like you told me to, but . . . that thing followed me."

"I am glad you are safe, Kevin," Gears said. He looked to the south and scanned the hills.

"What are you looking at?"

"Bumblebee and I received orders from General Marcus." Gears returned his gaze to Kevin. "Dr. Porter is preparing to launch a rocket carrying weapons that may endanger all Cybertronians, and the general needs our help to intervene. You should not stay here, Kevin. There may be more tanks. Reverb may have planned another wave of attacks."

"Last time I ran and hid," Kevin said, "it didn't work out so well. I'd probably be safer if I stayed with you."

"Agreed," Gears said with a nod. "Climb on my back. I must move quickly. And watch out for the heat exchangers on my back plate."

"I'll be careful," Kevin said, hoisting himself up onto Gears's shoulders. "Okay, I'm all set. Just one question. Where are we going?"

If Gears heard the question, he ignored it. He

was already running toward Hyperdynamix Aerospace.

Reverb stepped through the broken bits of metal that had been the main gates of the complex and ducked to avoid the red-hot edges of the hole his weapons had made. Behind him, Hyperdynamix guards lay writhing on the ground, their hands clapped over their ears.

Fire from Reverb's forearm cannons erupted as he entered the facility and strode through its cavernous interior. Thanks to the map of the complex that Stealth Leader had transmitted to him, he knew exactly which way to go. The main rocket-launch bay was directly ahead, and the control room was three levels above him.

Reverb sighted a team of soldiers to his right, and he growled as he turned to face them. They were carrying carbon-fiber weapons, which sprayed a refrigerated liquid that hardened when exposed to the air. Before the soldiers could attack, Reverb launched a pair of missiles at the ceiling above. They exploded, bringing large fragments of the ceiling down on the men. Reverb muttered, "Stupid insects."

He fired another pair of missiles at the doors to the main rocket-launch bay. The doors and the concrete wall that framed them exploded, spraying twisted shrouds of metal everywhere. Reverb marched through the fiery hole and saw Hyperdynamix technicians fleeing for the exits, abandoning the tall rocket located at the center of the large chamber. Reverb stomped into the bay and craned his neck to stare up at the rocket, its vents already hissing gases as it readied for liftoff.

Reverb considered firing a missile at the rocket but immediately dismissed the idea. He guessed the rocket contained nearly a million gallons of volatile fuel, which he suspected was enough to definitely blow him to bits, possibly level the mountainside, and maybe even destroy the entire complex.

"I gotta get to the control room," Reverb muttered. He mentally checked his map, tracing the route through freight elevators and corridors, and estimated that it would take four minutes to get to the control room. He had no doubt that soldiers would be guarding the premises.

"Begin final systems check," a voice boomed over the complex's public-address system. "Stand by for countdown."

"Countdown?!" Reverb said. Realizing that he might need a faster route to the control room, he looked up at the gantry that connected the rocket to the launching bay wall and spotted a glass window. From his map, he knew the control room was on the other side.

The Decepticon leaped for the gantry and began to climb, ascending the struts as if they were a gigantic jungle gym. He swiftly reached the control room's level and looked through the window.

The technicians on the other side looked in Reverb's direction and were startled. The Decepticon was pleased. He swung away from the gantry and crashed feetfirst into the window. He tumbled across the control room's floor and came to a stop in a kneeling crouch. The technicians scrambled for cover as Reverb unfolded his body and rose to his full height.

Reverb faced a man in a lab coat. "Dr. Porter, I presume," Reverb said. "I hear you're planning to use a signal from space to destroy all Decepticons. Well, that's not gonna happen."

Reverb expected the human to cower in fear and beg for his life, not respond with a smile as he pushed a button on a console beside him.

Sirens sounded. Over the noise, a voice from the loudspeaker announced, "Emergency launch sequence initiated. Three minutes to launch."

"Too late, Decepticon," Porter said. "Enjoy your final minutes before your long-overdue extinction."

Reverb's sonic weapon roared. Monitors exploded in showers of glass, while sparks and smoke erupted from every console in the control room. The blast hurled Porter and General Marcus against the wall with two sickening thuds. They lay on the floor, struggling to move.

Reverb moved toward Porter's slumped form, his metal fists clenched as he bellowed, "Cancel the countdown!"

Porter's eyes slowly rolled up to gaze at Reverb. He lifted one trembling arm, pointed at a smoking console, and then smiled again. "You just made that impossible."

"You stupid insect," Reverb snarled as he took another step toward the fallen men.

In the back of his family's helicopter, Douglas stared at his screen. Reverb's back shifted in front of the camera, blocking Douglas's view of his father and General Marcus. The Cybertronian shifted again, moving away from the camera, advancing toward—

Father!

Keeping his eyes on the screen, Douglas yelled, "How long until we reach Hyperdynamix Aerospace?"

"Twenty minutes, sir," the pilot said.

"Go faster!"

"We're at top speed now, sir."

On Douglas's screen, Reverb tore the ruined console from the floor and flung it behind him. The console struck the room's camera, and the window on Douglas's screen went black.

"No," Douglas muttered, shaking his head. "No. I didn't plan this. I didn't plan this...."

It was easy for Gears to figure out where Reverb had gone. The Autobot simply followed the trail of destruction from the highway to the Hyperdynamix Aerospace complex.

From atop Gears's back, Kevin said, "You're sure the Battle Mountain cylinder is safe?"

"As sure as I can be," Gears said as he moved past still-smoldering wreckage to enter the complex. "The cylinder appeared undamaged, and Bumblebee will stand guard over it until Optimus Prime arrives."

"Thank goodness," Kevin said.

They proceeded through the complex until they arrived at the main rocket-launch bay. Both looked up at the massive rocket, which stood beside a towering blast shield, and saw the bay's ceiling had been opened to the dark night sky. Kevin lowered his gaze, looked around the chamber, and noticed several overturned chairs and broken keypads lying on the floor. He said, "Looks like everyone left in a hurry. Any sign of Reverb?"

Gears scanned the gantry and noticed three slightly bent lengths of metal. Suspecting that Reverb may have caused the dents by using the gantry as a ladder, Gears looked higher until he spotted a shattered window.

"He must be up there," Gears said, striding toward the freight elevator. Kevin jumped down from his shoulders and ran alongside him.

As the elevator doors closed, a recorded voice announced from a loudspeaker, "Sixty seconds to launch."

The elevator rose rapidly to the third floor. Gears and Kevin leaped out and raced down the corridor to the control room. They found General Marcus and Lyons on their hands and knees, tending to the injured Dr. Porter.

Marcus looked up at Gears. His face was bleeding and covered with soot. "Reverb is on one of the rockets! You have to stop him!" Marcus pointed to the remains of the shattered window.

Gears and Kevin looked through the space previously occupied by the window. They saw a catwalk that led to a Reusable Launch Vehicle attached to a large rocket. Reverb was yanking at the heavy bolts that secured the RLV to the rocket's hull.

Kevin said, "Looks like he's trying to open the rocket's hatch, but his fingers are too big." From their new position on the third floor, Gears and Kevin could also see that the blast shield separated the rocket from a second rocket, which was hissing fumes.

Reverb noticed the Autobot, but knew Gears wouldn't dare try to shoot him while he was hanging on a highly explosive rocket. He laughed as he fired a single blast at the far end of the catwalk that had delivered him to the rocket. The catwalk's wall-mounted anchors fragmented, and the bridge fell to the bottom of the launch bay.

"Thirty seconds to launch," the recorded voice announced. And then the rocket's engines began to roar.

Lyons opened a thick metal door on the far side of the control room. "Into the safe room! Now! Or we'll be incinerated!"

Moving fast, Kevin ran back to General Marcus and helped him haul Dr. Porter to safety.

"Fifteen seconds," the recorded voice announced.

Gears kept his eyes on Reverb, who had locked his arms onto another set of mountings, pressing his body against the rumbling rocket.

"Ten seconds," the voice announced.

Gears started to climb out the window.

"Gears!" Kevin shouted from the safe room. "Get back here! You'll never make it!"

Gears hesitated and then turned away, racing from the ruined window and joining the humans in the safe room. Gears had no sooner sealed the metal door behind him than the entire complex began shaking. The massive rocket slipped free of its gantry and rode a pillar of flame toward space.

Porter gasped, "Is it away?"

"Yes, Dr. Porter," said Lyons.

"Excellent," Porter said as he closed his eyes. "I didn't tell that Decepticon savage the whole truth. The signal won't just fry his kind.... It will destroy every Cybertronian on Earth."

Marcus looked at Gears. Gears looked at

Kevin. Kevin's eyes went wide. "What?! But... the Autobots... they're our allies! Our friends!"

Porter opened his eyes again and fixed his gaze on Kevin. "Our kind can't be friends with the likes of those..." Porter shifted his gaze to Gears. "Those... *things*." He glanced at Marcus, who was kneeling beside him. "This will be *our* planet again. This... my final gift... to humanity. To my..."

Porter's eyes closed and his body went still. Lyons reached out to touch Porter's wrist. "I feel a pulse," Lyons said. "It's weak. We need a doctor!"

"Then call one!" General Marcus snapped.

Marcus faced Gears. "Gears, Porter programmed the second rocket to follow the first. Unless you do something..."

"Understood, General," Gears said. He rose, moved fast for the door, and flung it open.

"Wait for me!" Kevin yelled as he ran after Gears. Marcus shouted for Kevin to stop, but Kevin ignored him.

Gears stopped shy of the window that overlooked the launch room and said, "Kevin, you must stay back or—"

"You need me to get you into the RLV, Gears. Your fingers are like Reverb's... too big to open the hatch."

The recorded voice announced, "Sixty seconds to launch."

Gears said, "Kevin, I don't think you should—"

"You think you'll have a better chance of stopping Reverb if you ride that rocket into space on the *outside*?"

Before Gears could reply, Kevin jumped onto the Autobot's left knee, wrapped his arms tight around Gears's neck, then swung himself onto his back. "C'mon, Gears. Let's go!"

Gears ran for the ruined window, carrying Kevin with him. Gears kicked off from the window's lower frame and leaped for the RLV on the remaining rocket. Kevin gasped as Gears struck the RLV and bounced off, but landed on his feet on the gantry below the hatch.

"Thirty seconds to launch," said the recorded voice.

Gears held up Kevin. The human slipped his hands into a slot that held the hatch's locking controls and pressed a switch. A loud clack was followed by a hiss of air, and then the hatch swung open. Kevin jumped in. Gears quickly but carefully adjusted his shoulders, compressing them so he could squeeze through the hatch next.

"Fifteen seconds."

Gears sealed the hatch. Kevin found a cushioned seat and fell onto it, grabbing safety belts and tugging them across his chest and thighs. Gears braced himself against a cargo compartment.

From a speaker built into a console near Kevin's seat came General Marcus's voice. "Kevin! What the blazes do you think you're—"

Marcus's voice was lost as the rocket's engines ignited. The rocket rose up and out through the open ceiling and into the night sky.

Chapter Fourteen
LAUNCH

Duane had been keeping watch for several hours and hadn't seen any sign of predators. Several minutes after the planet's weak sun had begun to rise above the horizon, he ordered his men to move out.

Cobb sat up on the stony ground and rubbed his eyes. "Where to, Sarge?"

"Plan hasn't changed," Duane said. "We find our old fort, then we go to where we first arrived. Maybe there's something at the fort we missed.

And if not, it's a defensible position for the night. Better than this rock, at least."

Cobb nodded. Like the other soldiers, he looked exhausted. But Duane was proud of his men because they hadn't given up. And as long as he was alive, he would make sure they didn't.

They moved across the badlands single file, taking turns at point. Occasionally they heard the wolves howling in the distance, but they saw no sign of them. Duane wondered if they'd fled, if they'd been spooked by the centipedes. Or maybe they weren't in any hurry and were content to wait for night and better hunting.

He limped along with his soldiers, and they stopped every hour to eat and drink. By noon, they'd climbed out of the badlands into low, rolling hills. Ahead, on a rise, Duane spotted the spikes and spires of their first fort. The other soldiers saw it, too. Anson said, "At least we're getting to know our way around this planet. That's something, at least."

Rose said, "When the cavalry arrives, we can show them around, give them the grand tour."

McVey and Rose laughed at this. Duane said, "Keep your voices down. Save the laughs for when we get off this rock."

When they finally reached the fort, Duane allowed himself to sink wearily onto a pile of corroded green metal plates. As his squad drew up beside him, he said, "We'll search the area top to bottom. Look for machinery...anything resembling a map...anything we might be able to use."

Anson said, "We already did that, Sarge. That's why we left this fort. There was nothing useful here."

Duane looked up at Anson. His wounded arm was swollen.

"Would you rather lie down here and wait to

die, then, Corporal? Because while you're doing that, I'm going to keep looking for a solution to our problems."

Duane got to his feet and limped into the fort. A moment later, a grim-faced Anson joined him, and then all the soldiers began poking and sifting through the debris.

They searched for hours, pawing through hundreds of pounds of shattered alien machinery and building materials. Everything was broken, corroded, or turning into dust. Duane looked at the exhausted soldiers. He knew the last thing they needed was to sit around waiting for night and its terrors. Looking up through a hole in the ceiling, he saw the sun hanging lower in the sky, and said, "What would you guess, Rose? Four hours to sundown?"

Rose lifted his gaze to the ceiling's hole. "Seems about right to me, Sarge."

“All right then,” Duane said. “Our arrival point’s about an hour from here, along that dry riverbed. We’re going to go back there and perform the same search, see if we missed anything. We’ll take an hour, then return here for the night.” He looked at the other soldiers. “Everybody got that?”

They nodded. Duane wiped his brow.

“Everybody take a couple swigs of delicious tube-flower water, and let’s move out.”

The contrail from the second rocket was still a line of bright vapor when the helicopter touched the Hyperdynamix Aerospace landing pad. Douglas ducked beneath the whipping wash of the rotors, entered the building, and hurried to an elevator, which brought him to the auxiliary control room in less than a minute. Inside, he found General Marcus and Lyons.

They turned to the wild-eyed teenager. Marcus wore a bandage over his head, and his eyes looked tired. He walked over to Douglas, placed a hand on the boy's shoulder, and said, "Douglas, your father has been injured."

"I know," Douglas said as he stepped back, letting Marcus's hand fall away from his shoulder.

Marcus looked at the boy skeptically. "You know? But how could—"

"I heard," Douglas said quickly. "Where is my father?"

"We put him in the conference room," Marcus said. "I'll take you there if you'd like."

Douglas nodded mutely. Marcus walked slowly down the hall with him, keeping a short distance from the boy.

A NEST medical team was stationed beside Dr. Porter, who was lying on a wooden table, the lower half of his body covered by a sheet with a red H on it. Douglas realized the sheet was actually a drape his father had used to cover prototypes onstage before he would triumphantly unveil the latest inventions to the surprise and awe of his audience. His father had always seemed to take great pleasure in such events.

Douglas moved closer to his father. His father's mouth hung open slightly, and his left eyelid was twitching.

This isn't what I planned, Father.

Douglas said, "Will he live?"

"He's in bad shape," the medic leader said.

"But we have him stabilized. As soon as our transport team gets here, we'll take him straight to the hospital."

Marcus's phone chimed. He looked at it, then looked apologetically at Douglas. Douglas nodded and Marcus answered the call.

"Chief Lindsay? Yes, I understand. And we still have no idea what code to set? Uh-huh. Set up a one-hundred-foot perimeter around it, then. I'm not losing more people to that thing."

Douglas realized Chief Lindsay must have been telling General Marcus about the Cybertronian cylinder, which Douglas had regarded as the key to Project Nightbridge. He also realized the cylinder was possibly almost ready to activate. If it did, Kevin's brother would never come home. He remembered that Kevin had already lost his mother and father. Douglas glanced back at his own father.

He faced Marcus and said, "You're talking about the Cybertronian cylinder, the one from Battle Mountain."

Marcus's eyes went wide. "Just how would you know about that, son? And don't tell me you just 'heard' about that, too."

"Never mind about that right now," Douglas said. "I need to talk to Chief Lindsay. It's important."

Duane and his squad followed the dry riverbed to an area they remembered all too well. It was the hummock of red moss where they'd materialized after being spat out by the rip in space-time.

"Home sweet home," Rose said with a sardonic grin.

"Don't get too comfortable," Duane said. "All right, take a look around. When we were first here, we were too busy trying to figure out what had happened to really monitor our surroundings. Maybe we'll see something we missed."

"Like what, Sarge?" McVey asked.

"I don't know, McVey," Duane said. "You find a door that says THIS WAY TO EARTH, don't keep it to yourself. Anson, you're on watch. Make sure nothing sneaks up on us. The rest of you, turn over rocks, dig in the sand…do whatever needs doing to help get us out of here."

Cobb and McVey dug with their spears in the sand of the riverbed at various points, turning up all manner of odd alien shells, while Duane and Rose strained to turn over boulders, then worked to clear some of the moss away from the small promontory in the river. As they worked, the blue sun slowly sank. Duane reminded himself to keep track of the time. They'd die if they were caught in the open at night.

After much digging, Duane put his spear aside. He was exhausted, and it was nearly time to return to the fort. He decided to order his squad to rest for five minutes before they headed back.

And then what? Duane asked himself. *Come back here tomorrow? Wander the planet until we're eaten alive?*

He picked up his spear again and thrust it into the dirt in frustration. He was startled by the sound of metal on metal.

Rose heard it, too, and turned to see where Duane had stabbed his spear. Duane pulled his weapon out of the ground, and both men began scrabbling at the dirt with their hands. Rose said, "It might be just some buried junk."

"Only one way to find out," Duane said. The other soldiers saw the pair digging and came over to join them. Duane bent down and shoved a handful of dirt away from a long, slightly curved length of metal.

Cobb said, "Does that look like what I think it looks like?"

"Yes, it does," Duane said. "It's a cylinder. Like the one that sent us here. Keep digging."

Two minutes later, working carefully, the squad dug farther down and uncovered four rectangles along the side of the cylinder. Rose said, "Maybe it's a switch."

McVey looked at Duane and said, "Does it still work?"

Duane grinned. "How would I know? We have to examine it more—"

The four rectangles filled with yellow light and began flashing. Duane braced himself for what he believed would come next. But it didn't happen. He stood there with his squad, staring at the flashing rectangles.

Duane realized he'd been holding his breath, and he gasped as he said, "Something's happening. Something's definitely happening. I just wish I knew what it was!"

Chapter Fifteen
SATELLITE OF DOOM

Rising away from Earth, the rocket's third stage fell away, and the force pushing Kevin into his chair aboard RLV-3 diminished and then vanished completely, leaving him floating in the narrow confines of his harness. Through the cockpit's windows, he saw the darkness of outer space and the curve of Earth's hemisphere, a brilliant swirl of blues and whites.

Kevin turned his head to see Gears plastered

against a cargo compartment. "Are you all right?"

"Yes," Gears said as he carefully eased away from the compartment. "Zero gravity is actually quite comfortable."

The speaker on the console near Kevin pinged, and then a voice crackled to life on his radio. "We're glad to hear you two numbskulls are alive and well," said General Marcus. "Kevin, much as I'd like to lecture you about putting yourself in danger, we just don't have that kind of time. I'm turning you over to Mr. Lyons. He knows this equipment better than I do."

Kevin said, "But can we trust him? I mean, he works for Dr. Porter."

"If Lyons lies to us, I'll shoot him," Marcus said. Then he chuckled and added, "Just kidding. Here's Lyons. He says he has a job for you."

Lyons said, "Kevin, I hope you can operate some simple controls because...RLV-2 will automatically deploy the satellite. When it does, you'll have a chance to use RLV-3's manipulator arms to capture the satellite and deactivate it."

"Me?"

"Don't worry," Lyons said. "I'll talk you through the procedure. First, activate your control board. The autopilot is taking you directly to the HODDIS. You should see it in about ninety seconds."

"Where's Reverb?" Kevin said. "Did he survive?"

"RLV-2 is moving into position," Lyons said. "The satellite has been performing diagnostics as part of the normal deployment process. We don't have visual contact with it yet. You may see it before HODDIS can."

Kevin peered out the window and saw a brilliant speck ahead, hanging in the darkness above the Earth. "I see the space station now," he said. "And the RLV! But no sign of... wait a minute, I see him now. It's Reverb! He's on the outside of the RLV, trying to open the equipment bay."

Gears said, "I see him, too. I'll need to exit this vehicle."

"We'll need to depressurize the cockpit," Lyons said. "Kevin, there's a large compartment behind the seats that contains three emergency spacesuits. The smallest one might be a bit big for you, but you'll need to get into it. It's easy. There's an opening in the back of the suit, and the helmet is already attached. Just step into the opening, and the back of the suit will lock automatically."

Kevin opened the compartment, found the

smallest spacesuit, and climbed into it. He heard a series of clicks at his back as the locks secured and felt a rush of air around his body as the suit pressurized. He wiggled in the suit and had to crane his neck for a clear view through the helmet's visor.

Lyons said, "Kevin, your helmet has a built-in transmitter, so you should be able to hear me as well as Gears. All right, uh, Gears. You're clear to exit the RLV. Kevin, you should return to your seat."

Gears moved past the back of Kevin's seat, and the human said, "Gears, be careful out there."

Gears touched the top of Kevin's helmet and said, "I will do my best, Kevin." Gears went to the hatch, opened it, and shifted his body out of the RLV and onto its hull. The hatch closed behind him.

Reverb had never liked taking on the meteoroid form Cybertronians used for journeys between planets. To arrive on a world by plowing into its surface at high speed was inherently risky, and the energy demands of changing in and out of form left his reaction time diminished for days.

But in hindsight, he decided that method of travel was a lot better than hanging on to the side of a primitive rocket. His chassis had partially melted in several spots, dozens of sensors were alerting him to problems he couldn't fix, and his sensory inputs were struggling with phantom data.

With so many sensors malfunctioning, Reverb didn't believe his electronic eyes at first when he saw another RLV hurtling toward his spacecraft, with his old enemy Gears riding on top.

Reverb shifted his bulk hurriedly to the rear of RLV-2 and lifted his arm as he prepared to fire. The movement sent RLV-2 into a slow spin, and the craft fired its thrusters to compensate for the unexpected motion, throwing off Reverb's aim. His blast went wild into space.

Speaking over both a human and Cybertronian audio channel, Gears said, "We are not here to fight, Reverb. Kevin Bowman and I are here to help."

"Help me?" Reverb replied. "And why would you do that?"

"We know what your mission is," Gears said. "It's to stop the Hyperdynamix satellite. That's our mission, too."

"Liar," Reverb said. "What do you care if Decepticons get fried?"

"That satellite won't just fry Decepticons' circuits," Gears said. "It will destroy Autobots', too. Porter's goal was to extinguish all of our Sparks."

"What?!" snapped Reverb. "Of all the conniving... I should have killed him when I had the chance."

"Reverb, we have little time. You must believe me. The satellite will kill all Cybertronians on Earth."

Reverb snickered. "I believe you. You're too much of a goody-goody to lie. Enough talk, then." Reverb wrapped his knuckles against RLV-2's hull. "How do we crack open this insect toy?"

"We wait," Gears said. "After RLV-2 deploys the satellite, Kevin will grab it with RLV-3's manipulator arms and deactivate it."

"Kevin?" Reverb sneered. "Your pet? Never trust an insect to do a Cybertronian's job!"

Kevin said, "I can hear you, you know."

"Well, good for you," Reverb said. "You two

talk all you want. I'm not waiting!" The Decepticon began pounding on the hatch cover of RLV-2.

Kevin felt a bump as Gears launched himself from RLV-3, the Autobot's momentum carrying him across the short distance between the two spacecrafts. Gears reached out and grabbed one of RLV-2's manipulator arms.

Gears said, "Why, Reverb? Why do you always yield to foolish impulses?"

"Because unlike Autobots, I don't enjoy having others tell me what to do. Now, are you gonna keep preaching, or are you gonna help me break through this hatch?"

"Very well," Gears said. "We'll work together."

While Kevin hovered nearby in RLV-3, the two giant robots clung to the front of RLV-2 and used their free hands to hammer at the hatch cover. Gears managed to pry back part of it, then wedged his cannon into the gap he'd created. "Move aside, Reverb," he said. "I do not wish to accidentally damage you."

"I bet you might like to *deliberately* damage me," Reverb muttered as he scuttled to the rear of the spacecraft.

Gears opened fire. He could feel his arm cannons kicking, but the shots made no noise in the vacuum of space. RLV-2 began to tumble wildly and momentarily scrambled both Cybertronians' internal gyroscopes. Gears clung to the vehicle with both hands and waited for it to stabilize.

When Gears got his bearings, he was hanging from one of RLV-2's manipulator arms. He looked to his left and saw the blasted hatch cover tumbling through space as Reverb wedged into the RLV's exposed cockpit and cargo hold. As Gears twisted his body to get a better grip on the RLV, he saw Reverb remove a large silver sphere.

Seeing Reverb from his own spacecraft,

Kevin said, "Mr. Lyons, Reverb has Dr. Porter's satellite!"

Lyons's voice crackled, "Stick to the plan, Kevin! The satellite was engineered to resist intrusions."

Kevin said, "Reverb, stop! That's not going to work!"

"Quiet, larva," Reverb said. "Gears and I will both fire point-blank on the count of three—and cook Porter's toy."

The Decepticon released the satellite, and it began to drift away, floating serenely in front of the breached RLV-2. Gears and Reverb raised their right arms, hands shifting and changing into missile launchers. Reverb said, "One... two... *three*!"

The kick of the missile launch knocked RLV-2 and the two Cybertronians backward. Kevin peered out the window of RLV-3 and saw the satellite wobbling in space, its silvery sides dented and blackened.

"It wasn't destroyed," Kevin said, surprised. "Did those blasts knock it offline at least?"

Lyons responded, "We are performing diagnostics. Stand by." Several seconds later, Lyons continued, "The satellite is intact. Dr. Porter designed it with very thick armor. And what's more—"

Kevin watched as antennae extended from the sides of the satellite and lights began blinking around its perimeter. Kevin interrupted, "Uh, Mr. Lyons...the satellite just grew a bunch of antennae, and lights are flashing, and—"

"That's what I was about to tell you," Lyons said. "The satellite responded to the missile impact by accelerating the activation procedure. It's performing final diagnostic checks now."

Reverb snarled, "Now I'm really mad. Let's shoot the thing some more."

"Reverb, stop!" Kevin said. "You've done enough! Gears—"

"Kevin, listen," Lyons said. "You're going to need to go extravehicular."

"Extra-what?"

"You have to go outside the RLV. Your spacesuit has built-in thrusters that will let you maneuver. And under the console in front of you, there's a tool kit you can strap around your arm."

Gears said, "I will assist you, Kevin."

Kevin looked at the distance between the two RLVs and said, "I don't know how you can help, Gears. Just keep Reverb from doing anything stupid."

Kevin found the tool kit and strapped it to the forearm of his spacesuit, then followed Lyons's instructions to depressurize the cockpit and open the hatch. Kevin unstrapped himself from the operator's chair in the RLV and floated. He thought, *It's almost like swimming.*

Moving outside the RLV, he looked past his feet to see Earth, blue and welcoming. Turning his head slightly, he saw the Moon as a white orb. He felt very small, as if he were a speck of dust adrift in the universe.

Still listening to Lyons, Kevin tapped the controls for his thrusters to orient his body so he faced the satellite. He tapped the controls again and accelerated smoothly forward. Beyond the satellite, he saw Gears and Reverb clinging to the sides of RLV-2, glaring at each other.

Lyons said, "You're doing great, Kevin. Right on target. Don't fire the thrusters again. There's nothing to slow you down in space."

The satellite appeared to grow larger as

Kevin moved closer to it. He stretched out his arms to cushion the impact as he smacked into it and managed to grab hold of an antenna.

Gears said, "Are you all right, Kevin?"

"Fine," Kevin said.

Lyons said, "Make your way around to the back access panel. Take your time."

Kevin found the access panel and said, "How much time do I have?"

"Don't be nervous," Lyons said. "It's a delicate operation, but I'm, uh, sure you can handle it."

Something in the tone of the technician's voice made Kevin suspicious. "Just tell me... how much time before the satellite is set to transmit its signal?"

"Six minutes," Lyons said.

Kevin gasped, "Six minutes?!"

The NEST military copter kicked up a blinding cloud of dust as it set down beside Highway 99. The towering figure of Optimus Prime emerged and surveyed the scene before him. Wrecked trucks and military vehicles—some still burning—were strewn across the highway. Optimus let his gaze sweep over them, then the twisted, broken tanks that had attacked the NEST convoy.

Ironhide and Ratchet moved behind Optimus as Bumblebee rushed to meet them. Chief Lindsay, who had to hurry to keep up with the yellow-and-black Autobot, followed.

"You have done well, Bumblebee. Did our forces manage to track the fleeing Hyperdynamix tanks?" Optimus asked.

Bumblebee let out an electronic squall of enthusiasm.

Lindsay reported on the situation, "Although

protecting the Battle Mountain cylinder remains our top priority, General Marcus assigned several squads to pursue the tanks. The squad leaders have reported that they managed to plant tracking devices. We'll be able to find them all and bring them down if necessary. But...did General Marcus inform you about Dr. Porter's satellite—and what's happening in orbit right now?"

"Yes, General Marcus briefed me," Optimus said. "Are Gears and Kevin Bowman all right?"

"Last I heard, they were still attempting to deactivate the satellite."

Optimus looked up at the stars overhead. "I suppose if they fail, every Cybertronian on Earth will know soon enough." Lowering his gaze to Lindsay, he continued, "There is nothing more we can do but wait. What is the status of the cylinder?"

"We've ordered all personnel to retreat to

outside a protective perimeter. We don't know exactly how long it will be until the cylinder activates, but I doubt it will be more than two hours."

From behind Lindsay, a voice called out, "Less than that, I'm afraid."

The Autobots and Lindsay turned to see Douglas Porter walking along the highway, carrying his notebook. With him were a Hyperdynamix technician and one of General Marcus's aides.

Optimus thought the teenager looked not only exhausted but also as if he'd aged several years in a very short time. "Douglas," Optimus said. "I am sorry your father was injured."

Ratchet bowed his head to Douglas and said, "I have training in post-traumatic therapeutics. Please let me know if I can be of assistance."

Ironhide felt obliged to make some gesture to Douglas, but all he could muster was a respectful dip of his battle-scarred metal chin.

"Thank you," Douglas said. His lower lip trembled. "I'm sorry. I really don't deserve your sympathy. I...I was angry with my father for a very long time. And I haven't been honest with you."

Optimus said, "What do you mean?"

Douglas stepped over to a half-crushed car and propped his computer on the back of it. Lindsay and the Autobots moved up behind him, so they could see the screen. "This is drone footage from the fight at Hawthorne Army Depot, where Kevin's brother disappeared."

Chief Lindsay watched in fascination as the first several seconds of the video played out, and then said, "How did you get this...? Wait! Go back....Freeze that frame! Can you enhance that?"

Douglas nodded. "That's the readout on the

trans-spatial Cybertronian cylinder. I know it's the key to having any chance of rescuing Sergeant Bowman and the rest of his squad." Douglas showed an enhanced view of the readout. "There. You can see the Cybertronian numbers perfectly."

"This is the code we need!" Lindsay said, his eyes bright with excitement. "Optimus, I have to reset the cylinder!"

Optimus said, "I know trans-spatial porting was abandoned because it was unsafe. But there is much that we do not know. What if resetting the cylinder opens a portal to the center of a star? We could be endangering many more lives than our own."

Douglas said, "But consider the cylinder at Hawthorne. It opened a wormhole that closed within seconds. If we could repeat that with the Battle Mountain cylinder, it could be our best and only chance to save Kevin's brother."

"If Kevin's brother is still alive," Optimus said.

"I want to help, Optimus," Douglas said. "I confess I didn't tell anyone about this video because I wanted to use it for myself, to make my father look bad. I wanted his attention. I wanted him to notice me. I wanted him...to love me."

Douglas snuffled. His eyes began to tear, and he reached up to drag his sleeve across his face. "I'll reset the cylinder. If I die, let it be some repayment for my bad decisions."

"I am not risking the life of a child," Optimus said, "even one who has proved his bravery by telling the truth."

Chief Lindsay said, "I believe I'm capable of resetting the cylinder. Douglas, could you please send that image to my phone?"

"Of course," Douglas said. "I'll send it

to Kevin's as well. I believe he'll want to see it, too."

Ironhide kicked one foot in the ground and muttered, "I just hope Kevin and Gears stop that satellite so I can keep on living and fighting Decepticons!"

Chapter Sixteen

BETRAYAL IN OUTER SPACE

Kevin pulled himself hand over hand across the curved surface of the satellite. He tried not to look down at Earth.

Reverb growled, "Hurry up, brat."

"Why don't you shut up already?" Kevin replied. He maneuvered his body beside the satellite's rear access panel. Hanging on to an antenna with one hand, Kevin extracted a powered wrench from his tool kit. He fitted the wrench over the head of a bolt and activated it. The satellite jerked briefly before the bolt began to spin off.

Kevin had forgotten that mission control was monitoring his movements and was startled when he heard Lyons say, "Don't let the bolt drift away! We don't want any more dangerous debris floating around in orbit."

Kevin removed the bolt carefully and tucked it into a pocket on his spacesuit. There were three bolts left. He set his wrench and removed the second bolt, then got to work on the third, taking care to tuck each bolt into his pocket. He took a deep breath and fit the wrench over the last bolt.

The bolt spun halfway out of its threads, then jammed. Surprised, Kevin almost lost his grip on the antenna. Flailing to regain his grip, he accidentally released the wrench.

"Gears!" he yelped. "Help!"

Lyons said, "What's wrong, Kevin?"

"I lost the wrench!"

Gears said, "I see it, Kevin. I will get it." Gears pushed off from RLV-2. From Kevin's point of view, Gears appeared to fly through the darkness of space toward the tumbling wrench.

"Lyons!" Kevin yelled as he clung to the satellite's antenna. "How much time?"

"Two minutes," Lyons replied grimly.

"Unbelievable," Reverb muttered. "Sentenced to death by the clumsiness of a half-grown larva."

Gears said, "Silence, Reverb." The Autobot reached out and caught the wrench and then tried to turn his body, but with nothing to stop him, he continued moving along his original trajectory.

"Gears!" Kevin said. "Use your missile launcher! Fire it in the opposite direction of where you want to go!"

Gears extended his arm, reshaping it. He looked over his shoulder at Kevin, and then fired. The blast sent him flying back toward the satellite and the two RLVs.

"Ninety seconds," Lyons announced.

"Gears!" Kevin yelled. "Throw the wrench to me!"

Gears drew back his arm and let the wrench fly. Kevin watched it spin toward him. He pulled himself up on the antenna, reaching as high as he could. The wrench touched his fingers and spun off to one side. Within a flash it was already five feet away.

"Idiot!" Reverb howled.

Lyons said, "One minute."

Kevin gave the wrench a despairing look and then turned back to the satellite. The final bolt on the access panel was halfway out of its slot. He took a deep breath, braced his legs on the antennae, fit his thick-gloved fingers awkwardly over the bolt, and tried to turn it.

Kevin tried to get a better grip. "C'mon," he muttered. And then the bolt turned. He gave it another twist, and it turned again. He repeated the action until the bolt came free, quickly tucked the bolt in his pocket, and pulled the access panel away from the satellite.

"Lyons!" Kevin yelled. "What am I looking for?"

"Three red wires," Lyons said. "Pull them out of their sockets."

The satellite began to vibrate, lights blinking in neat lines around its middle. Kevin said, "The satellite is shaking. What's happening?"

"The broadcast sequence is starting," Lyons said. "Thirty seconds, Kevin."

Kevin looked into the satellite's guts and saw bundles of wires everywhere. To his horror, all of them were coated with a layer of white frost. He couldn't tell red from any other color.

The satellite continued to vibrate, and the blinking lights began flashing faster and more brightly. Kevin brushed his gloves over the wires, wiping away the frost.

Black wire... black wire... green wire... red wire—*red!* He found two more red wires.

A light came on inside the satellite. Kevin grabbed the three red wires in his fist, braced his feet against the satellite's side, and pulled the wires as hard as he could. The effort pushed him away, leaving him tumbling head over heels in space. As he tried to stop himself from spinning, he yelped, "Did that work? Did I—"

He bumped up against something hard, and the impact jarred his teeth. Turning his head so he could see what he'd hit, he saw Gears.

Gears said, "I fired my cannon again to maneuver myself to catch you. Are you all right?"

"Fine," Kevin said. "Did I stop the satellite?"

Gears looked at the satellite and said, "If it did transmit a signal, I am unaffected. My primary systems remain operational."

Kevin turned his head again to look at Reverb, who was still clinging to RLV-2. Kevin said, "What about you, Reverb?"

Reverb said, "I guess you didn't screw up, insect."

Lyons said, "You did it, Kevin! The satellite is inoperative. Great job."

Kevin grinned, then glanced over Gears's shoulder. Reverb had launched himself off RLV-2 and was soaring silently toward the two of them. Then Kevin noticed that Reverb's forearm had reconfigured itself into a missile launcher.

"Gears!" Kevin yelled. "Look out!"

Before Gears could turn, Reverb fired. The missile caught Gears in the back, causing the Autobot to release Kevin and sending Gears spinning like a top. Blobs of melted metal fell away from Gears's back. His once-radiant blue eyes dimmed as he turned, trying to reach for Reverb.

Kevin screamed, *"No!"*

Reverb reformed his forearms into cannons and aimed them at Kevin. "Now it's your turn, insect."

Kevin looked from the horrible grin on Reverb's metal face to the Decepticon's blaster cannons. "I saved your life!"

"And I'll return the favor by ending yours," Reverb gloated. "Just hold still! I don't want to waste any ammo on—"

A black sphere came from out of nowhere and hit Reverb in the midsection, knocking him sideways and spoiling his aim. Reverb fired, sending a missile toward Earth's atmosphere. Reverb snarled. "What hit me?" As he tilted his head to look at his lower body, another black sphere hit him in the side of the head.

"Ouch!" Reverb cried. A third black sphere crashed into his knees.

Kevin saw more spheres traveling toward his position and assumed they would strike him, too. As he braced himself to be hit, he was surprised to hear a new voice emit from his helmet's radio. "Hang in there, kid. We've got your back."

Lyons said, "HODDIS crew, is that you?"

"That's a roger. Commander Gent speaking. We saw what was happening and figured our drones could be useful. After all, it's our job to clean up space trash."

Reverb snarled and fired his cannons, blasting

one of the drones into pieces. The other drones swarmed the furious Decepticon, and Kevin realized the HODDIS astronauts were controlling the drones, making them dodge and weave around Reverb, taking turns to dart in and smash into him. As Kevin watched, the drones drove Reverb farther and farther away, sending him closer to Earth and returning him to the planet's gravitational pull. The Decepticon's flailing figure appeared to dwindle in size, becoming a small black dot before it entered Earth's atmosphere and ignited.

Commander Gent said, "You okay, kid?"

"Yes, but Gears is...I think he might have been destroyed." Kevin fired his spacesuit's thrusters and traveled to his friend's side. He reached out to touch Gears's broad metal forehead.

Gears's eyes flickered.

Kevin said, "Gears? *Gears!*" Kevin thought

he heard something over his earpiece, a low buzz that might have been a word. "Gears, did you say something?"

In a low, mechanical whisper, Gears said, "Repairable."

Kevin heard the HODDIS astronauts cheer. Then Lyons said, "Kevin, General Marcus says there's something you need to know about. He says to tell you they've found the code for the cylinder. I assume that means something to you?"

"Yes, it does," Kevin said. "Did General Marcus mention the cylinder's countdown, how much time is left?"

"The general says he doesn't know," Lyons said. "But he wants you back here. Your RLV's autopilot can bring you home."

"But what about Gears?"

Commander Gent replied, "We'll use the drones to bring him aboard HODDIS and send him back with the next equipment shuttle. Go on home, kid. And don't worry about Gears."

Kevin looked at Gears and said, "See you soon, pal." Then he fired his spacesuit's thrusters and streaked back to RLV-3.

Chapter Seventeen
HOMEWARD BOUND

Despite Kevin's doubts, returning to Earth in the RLV really was as simple as Lyons had said. He sealed the hatch, strapped himself into his seat, gave the little craft's onboard computer a few instructions, and the RLV fired its thrusters to enter a long, slow curving trajectory back into Earth's atmosphere.

Kevin watched through the cockpit window in awe as Earth grew larger and larger. Then the sky faded from black to a dark blue as RLV-3 fell closer to Earth.

At first, the bumps were gentle and Kevin's descent was gradual. But within a few minutes, the RLV was jouncing and the view through the cockpit was tinged red and yellow by the heat of the craft's passage through the atmosphere. Kevin was sure Reverb could not survive such intense heat during his own descent to Earth, and all he could do was trust that the RLV would remain intact for the rest of the trip.

Then the RLV stopped shaking, and Kevin looked through the window to see he was hurtling over the Atlantic Ocean. He said, "Lyons? Do you read me? Am I on course?"

"Looking great, Kevin," Lyons said. "RLV-3 is programmed to land right here at Hyperdynamix. Should have you on the ground in about five minutes."

Kevin saw the east coast of North America below him. He said, “Can General Marcus make sure someone can bring me to the cylinder?”

“A NEST driver will take you to the cylinder, Kevin, right after a routine postmission physical exam.”

“What?” Kevin was moving over the central U.S., and the RLV was beginning to slow. “Forget about a physical. There’s no time!”

“Standard safety protocols,” Lyons said patiently, “call for a physical exam after spaceflight and reentry. Should only take an hour or so.”

Ignoring Lyons, Kevin examined the RLV’s console and started thumbing through computerized menus. He searched until he found a way to call up a map of his location and the menu for switching between autopilot and manual control.

Mission City was a glowing grid below the RLV now, with Las Vegas a brighter, multicolored blaze of illumination ahead. A minute later, the RLV's retrorockets fired, and the map showed that he was descending toward Hyperdynamix Aerospace. Highway 99 was a bright thread just west of the red H on his screen.

Lyons said, "You're on course for a perfect descent, Kevin. Our physicians are standing by."

Kevin looked at the pilot's joystick uncertainly. He pushed the on-screen button for manual control as he shifted his feet to touch the brake and accelerator pedals.

"Kevin," Lyons said, "don't be alarmed, but you've accidentally switched control to manual."

"Sorry about that," Kevin said. "Tell the doctors my checkup will have to wait." He pushed the joystick forward, ignoring Lyons's protests, and the RLV zipped ahead. The Spring Mountains passed by below. Kevin dipped the craft, braking gently. He could see a circle of lights below him blazing brightly.

"Kevin!" Lyons said. "I don't know what you're doing but...Douglas Porter wishes to speak with you."

Douglas?

"Kevin, Douglas here. I have a lot to explain to you, but before I do, I want you to know I just sent an image file to your cell phone. It's a close-up of the cylinder Reverb used at Hawthorne. You'll find it—"

"Sorry, Douglas," Kevin said. "But I'm kind of trying to land without getting killed right now." He switched off the radio so he wouldn't be distracted, then found the controls for the RLV's external cameras. He was descending toward the trucks and vehicles that had been destroyed in the battle with Reverb. He saw a wide circle of lights surrounding one of the destroyed trucks. Within the circle there were bits of wreckage, but no people that he could see.

Perfect spot for a landing, Kevin thought. He tapped the brakes and brought RLV-3 down toward the center of the area ringed by lights. He spotted a few tall figures and realized he was looking at Optimus Prime, Ironhide, Ratchet, and Bumblebee, who were standing a short distance from the truck that had carried the Cybertronian cylinder. Bumblebee waved at him.

And then Kevin saw a bright flash of light. He closed his eyes.

Bumblebee was still waving as Kevin and the RLV vanished in midair.

Chapter Eighteen
REUNITED

Duane and the rest of his squad stared at the top of the alien cylinder sticking out of the ground. The four glass rectangles on the cylinder kept flashing yellow.

Duane said, "Anybody have any ideas about what this does, or how it works?" He looked at his men and saw in their expressions equal parts anxiety and hope.

Anson said, "Sorry, Sarge, but...for all we

know, that device could be anything from a transporter to a time bomb."

Duane said, "Well, we could go back to the fort for the night, and we'd probably be safer there than we are here, at least from the wolves. But if we survive the night and come back tomorrow and find that this thing is gone and we somehow lost our only ticket home...what's it going to be, men? Stay here or back to the fort?"

Anson said, "I'm for staying right here."

"Me too, Sarge," Cobb said. The others nodded in agreement.

"All right then," Duane said. "I'll try touching it. Maybe it has some concealed, easy-to-read instructions." Duane grinned, and the other soldiers laughed.

He stepped close to the cylinder and placed his right hand on it, just beside the illuminated glass rectangles. "It's warm," Duane said. Just then a power surge rushed through the cylinder, and Duane flew backward and crashed against the ground.

Duane rolled over and blinked his eyes, and when he regained his vision, he wondered if his eyes were deceiving him.

A small spacecraft was floating a few feet above the riverbed. It settled onto the loose sand with a bump, its engines whining as they shut down. The soldiers fanned out, their spears held at the ready.

A hatch opened, and a small figure in a silver spacesuit emerged. Duane took a tentative step forward, trying to peer through the dark visor of the figure's helmet. He heard a muffled voice say, "Duane!"

"Kevin?" Duane said in disbelief.

Kevin reached up to the helmet's locking mechanisms, unlocked them, and removed his helmet. "Duane! I don't believe it! I...I found you!"

As the soldiers gaped, Duane and the boy in the gleaming spacesuit hugged, staring at each other in happy amazement. Smiling broadly, Duane looked at his men and said, "My brother! My brother's here!" And then Duane held Kevin at arm's length and said, "Kevin... how did...what are you doing here?"

"I'm not sure, exactly," Kevin said. He looked around. "And where is 'here'? I mean, where are we?" Before Duane could answer, Kevin slapped himself on his forehead. "The cylinder! It was in the circle where I was landing."

Cobb said, "Uh, just what the heck are you talking about?"

Kevin said, "I was landing in Nevada, and the Cybertronian cylinder must have activated just as I was passing it, or...maybe I triggered it somehow." Kevin looked past the other soldiers and saw a familiar-looking object with four glass rectangles on it. "Another cylinder."

Duane said, "Kevin, I can't believe you're here, but maybe if you just calm down, you can explain how you—"

Just then there was a sound of metal legs clattering over rocks.

Kevin said, "What was that?" The noise seemed to be multiplying around them.

"Oh no," Duane said.

Kevin turned and saw the centipedes. They had the soldiers surrounded.

"Everyone quiet," Duane whispered. "Remember, they're blind."

The beasts moved closer to the soldiers, and a few jumped up on their rear legs and moved their heads back and forth, as if they were sniffing the air.

Rose said, "They know we're here."

"I think you're right," Duane said.

One centipede moved up beside the RLV, shifted its body, and struck the RLV hard enough to send it skidding across the ground. The RLV's hatch remained open like a gaping mouth.

Duane said, "Kevin, I don't suppose you came with a plan for getting back home, or have a way to call for reinforcements."

"Well," Kevin said, "getting *here* wasn't exactly planned, and I doubt my phone will get reception from wherever we...hang on! My phone!"

"Your phone?" Duane said. "Seriously?"

Kevin tore at the fastenings of his spacesuit, fumbling out of it to free his hands so he could reach his cell phone in his pants pocket. As the robots clacked their jaws and moved closer to Duane's group, Duane said, "Whatever you're going to do, Kevin, do it fast."

Kevin activated his phone and prayed it had automatically downloaded the image file that Douglas had sent. He swiped at the screen and found the photo. He gasped. It was a close-up of the Cybertronian numbers on the cylinder Reverb had used during the battle at Hawthorne.

One of the centipedes screeched as it swung its tail and its stinger swept dangerously close to the soldiers. Kevin leaped beside the pillar and examined the glyphs displayed on its glass rectangles, then held up his phone to quickly compare the glyphs with the ones displayed in the photo Douglas had sent. They matched.

Kevin looked at the switch to the right of the readouts, the one Lindsay had decided set the countdown on the pillar. Kevin remembered Lindsay had moved the switch clockwise to increase the power level and wondered if the cylinder before him operated the same way.

Only one way to find out. Kevin turned the switch slightly clockwise and heard it click as the centipedes screeched and charged.

Optimus Prime knew that a good leader was often required to keep emotions in check. No one had been able to prevent Kevin Bowman from landing within the perimeter around the Cybertronian pillar and no one knew anything about where Kevin might have gone. Optimus understood that accidents and mistakes happened, but it took a great deal of concentration for him to remain calm and not reveal his anger at those who had allowed Kevin to vanish.

Standing outside the Cybertronian cylinder's perimeter near the Hyperdynamix Aerospace complex, Optimus looked down at Chief Lindsay and Douglas Porter and said, "Anything new to report, Chief Lindsay?"

"Power levels are steady since the spike when the cylinder activated," Lindsay said. "The cylinder still seems intact and functional, which is different from what happened to the one Reverb used at Hawthorne. But that's about all I can tell you."

Behind Optimus Prime, Ironhide shifted back and forth impatiently beside Ratchet and Bumblebee. Ratchet said, "I still say we go after the kid."

Bumblebee hopped up and down and emitted a burst of pop music to encourage Optimus. Optimus turned to face his fellow Autobots and said, "What if the cylinder sent Kevin into the middle of an asteroid field or to the periphery of a black hole? What then? Shall I lose another friend and ally, too? It grieves me to say it, but we will wait. We will wait until we—"

"Optimus!" yelled Lindsay. "Power levels are spiking!"

Anticipating a possible attack, the Autobots raised their arms, metal limbs reshaping themselves into blaster cannons and missile launchers. The NEST commandos brought their machine guns to their shoulders, ready to fire.

A brilliant flash of light burst a few feet away from the Cybertronian cylinder, and then six figures—a boy and five men—materialized and came stumbling across the highway. Optimus recognized Kevin and the soldiers who had vanished at Hawthorne, and he bellowed to his troops, "Hold your fire!"

"Watch out!" Kevin shouted as he and the five soldiers ran toward the Autobots. "We've got monsters right behind us!"

"Outta the way!" bellowed Ironhide as he

strode forward with his missile launcher raised. "Let's blast that infernal cylinder to slag!"

"No!" yelled Douglas Porter, who'd remained beside Chief Lindsay. "You don't need to do that! Just reset the cylinder's coordinates! That will sever the link and close the portal!"

Before anyone could stop him, Douglas ran onto the highway and stopped before the cylinder. He twisted the switch to the left and tapped at the glass rectangles, changing the numerals displayed. "We're safe," Douglas said. He turned to face Kevin and the five ragged looking soldiers.

Kevin said, "I appreciate that you sent me that image file, Douglas, but I'm curious... how did you get that photo?"

Douglas said, "I have a lot to explain."

"Yes, Douglas," Optimus Prime said. "You do."

Chapter Nineteen
MISSION ACCOMPLISHED

At the NEST Rapid Response Base, General Marcus sat in a conference room with Chief Lindsay and a crowd of aides and soldiers, while Optimus Prime, Ironhide, Ratchet, and Bumblebee stood against the wall.

"Let's review what we know," General Marcus said. "Sergeant Bowman has confirmed that the robot centipedes he encountered on the so-called Blue Planet are identical to the ones we fought in Idaho."

"Correct," Optimus said. "Clearly there was a link between the two. But this defies logic. While we do not know the location of Blue Planet, it must be several light-years away from Earth. To reach Earth when they did, the centipedes would have had to leave Blue Planet long before Sergeant Bowman and his squad ever arrived there."

Marcus glowered. "But we didn't detect the centipedes until they were nearly in our orbit. Our early-warning systems should have seen them long before that. What does that tell us?"

Optimus said, "It suggests that the invaders arrived here by using other trans-spatial portals, portals connecting Blue Planet with a point beyond the orbit of the Moon."

Marcus said, "Should we expect more invaders from Blue Planet?"

"We shall remain watchful," Optimus said,

"but I believe they no longer pose a threat. It is my assessment that our discovery of the Cybertronian cylinders may have somehow alerted the invaders to the location of Earth, but that their data about the location was lost when the cylinder from Battle Mountain was deactivated."

Chief Lindsay said, "That's my conclusion as well. The invaders may have found us by chance if not by some ancient plan, but without an open link to interspatial portals...well, outer space is incredibly vast and constantly expanding. And from the way Sergeant Bowman described his experience on Blue Planet, it doesn't sound like the beasts are building an armada."

Optimus said, "So long as no one enters Blue Planet's coordinates into the Battle Mountain cylinder, the beasts cannot find us."

Marcus looked to Chief Lindsay and said, "What is the status of the Battle Mountain cylinder?"

"We've moved it to the Yucca Mountain vault, where it's being observed under heavy guard. We're reviewing Douglas Porter's notes on the technology, the notes from his files that he gave us."

"You mean the files that 'Stealth Leader' gave us?" General Marcus shook his head sadly. "That poor, rich, brilliant, and twisted Douglas Porter. It just busts me up that a boy with his brains would be so vengeful that he'd go to such incredible lengths to bring down his father's company and ruin him."

Optimus said, "Blame should not be placed solely on Douglas's shoulders. Had Dr. Porter ever shown his son any kindness, I believe Douglas would have been a better, stronger person. And let us all bear in mind that after his father was injured, Douglas did choose to *help* us."

"He did help," Marcus said, "but he also caused a lot of damage."

"General, I realize you may be inclined to press charges against Douglas Porter, but I believe there is good in him and that more good will come if we help him."

"I'll certainly consider that," Marcus said. "Now, on to another subject. How is Gears?"

Ratchet replied, "Gears was very fortunate that his Spark was not extinguished. His systems are repairing themselves. He is on leave at the moment, but he will be able to return to duty in a couple weeks."

"Excellent," Marcus said. "And what about Reverb? Any sign of him?"

Ratchet said, "My assumption is that he burned up in the atmosphere."

"Let's not make any assumptions," Marcus said. "He survived the trip into space, after all. Let's send out a detachment to conduct a search around his likely point of reentry."

"Anything else?" Marcus said. "No? Well, gentlemen, we have had a brush with disaster, a disaster we escaped because of the bravery of one boy and the last-minute honesty of another. But so long as the Decepticons remain a threat, our world is still in danger. We have a lot of work to do, so let's get to it!"

Kevin Bowman gently tapped at the door to the hospital suite. The door opened and

Douglas Porter quietly ushered Kevin into the room. His father was lying on a bed, surrounded by medical equipment and beeping computer monitors. Kevin whispered, "How is he?"

"He talked for a while yesterday," Douglas said. "He knows what happened and where he is. Thanks for coming here."

"No, thank you. Without that picture you sent me—"

"Please don't thank me," Douglas said as he gazed down at his sleeping father. "I spent my whole life angry about my father, and it wasn't until he was almost killed that I realized just how selfish I'd been. I…I just want you to know I'm sorry for all the terrible things I did, and I'm glad Duane and his squad are all right," Douglas said.

Dr. Porter let out a long sigh and opened his

eyes. Douglas leaned closer to him and said, "Father? Can you hear me?"

Porter raised a trembling hand and held it out to his son. As Douglas took it, his father said, "We'll…we'll get through this, son."

Douglas's eyes began to tear. Kevin said, "I, uh…I'll be going now. Take care." He turned and walked out of the room quietly, leaving the father and son behind.

Kevin walked out of the hospital and returned to the parking lot, where an armored truck was waiting for him. He climbed up into it and let out a long sigh as he sank against the passenger seat.

From the truck's radio, Gears said, "Are you all right, Kevin?"

"Yeah, I'm okay," Kevin said as he buckled in. "I used to really envy Douglas, but now... now I just feel sorry for him. I hope he and his father can work things out."

Gears was silent for a moment, then he said, "You are a good friend, Kevin Bowman."

"Thanks, Gears. Same to you."

"I'll miss you when I return to NEST headquarters."

"Don't get all weepy on me just yet." Kevin laughed. "You don't have to return for two weeks. So, what should a boy and an Autobot do to celebrate after they've helped save the world?"

"Hmm," Gears said. "Want to go for a drive?"

"Sure," Kevin said. "Let's roll."